"An exceptional book, a real fai...
An enthralling multi-layered w..........fantasy
with a deep, dark heart lurking beneath the
surface."
Ginger Nuts of Horror

"It had a whimsical, Neil Gaiman-esque quality
(and since I worship Neil Gaiman, this is very
high praise). Lovely, somewhat lyrical, the writing was wonderful."
Bellsie Books

"The whole experience was like reading from
inside the Mad Hatter and Cheshire Cat's brain
combined. Everything was just slightly off-
kilter and I loved every minute of it."
In Pursuit of My Own Library

"A penny dreadful fairy tale – delightfully dark,
wonderfully wicked, highly original! 5 stars."
Views & Reviews

"This will probably be ranking as one of my
favorite books of the year... I loved every
minute of it."
From My Bookshelf

• ISHBELLE BEE •

The Contrary Tale of the

BUTTERFLY GIRL

from
THE PECULIAR ADVENTURES
OF JOHN LOVEHEART, ESQ.
VOL. II

ANGRY
ROBOT

ANGRY ROBOT
An imprint of Watkins Media l

Lace Market House,
54-56 High Pavement,
Nottingham,
NG1 1HW
UK

angryrobotbooks.com
twitter.com/angryrobotbooks
Prime suspect

An Angry Robot paperback original 2015
1

A catalogue record for this book is available
from the British Library.

ISBN 978 0 85766 444 0
EBook ISBN 978 0 85766 446 4

Set in Meridien and more by Argh! Nottingham.
Illustrations by John Coulthart.
Printed by 4edge Ltd.

For Tom x

"REVENGE
SHOULD HAVE NO BOUNDS."

William Shakespeare, *Hamlet*, IV.vii

butterfly
butterfly
butterfly

butter-fly

BUTTER **FLY** **FLY** **FLY**

butterfly

butterfly

My name is Izel. I am a warrior woman.

My soul is a butterfly.

I am the last of my people.

They were sacrificed to a mad sorcerer; hearts ripped out, beating in his hands. He ate them, one after another.

What did they taste of, I wonder? Something sticky, something hot. Put them in a pie, arrange them on an altar. Line them up on display. Red after red.

Does he lick his fingers or wipe them on his robes?

Does he know I'm coming for him?

I am a collector of heads. I'm going to put his on a stick. Stuff his mouth with the names of my people.

They say a butterfly is the soul of a warrior. They say when I am dead I will fly over this beautiful land, spread my wings. Glide on ghost wings.

Give me a good death; give me some meaning. Let me write my name in blood across his temple, smear it into the walls. Leave a hand print; five fingers of a star. Mark him.

I wear a butterfly tattoo of the Angel-Eater: black wings, red eyes. It is a predator; for it eats its own kind. It was carved on my back by a priest. He told me, "This will hurt. Revenge always does." He chanted over my body, said prayers at my feet. Entwined animal bones and exotic purple flower-weeds in my hair. Charms for protection; help from the gods.

The mad sorcerer's black temple of butterflies is soaked in blood. So many steps, they reach to the gods. My people's bodies rolled down those steps. Bounced to the bottom.

The sorcerer wears a mask of butterflies, lightning blue and gold. Five hundred acolytes kneel before him: black robed with curved silver daggers. Hypnotised by his magic. They pray at his temple, mad-eyed, their mouths full of star shapes. Galactic poison seeps in their veins like plant tendrils, shifts and coils beneath their skin.

I am unique for a woman, for I am six feet tall; taller than any man. My hair, which is black, reaches to my bottom; it is entwined with tiny animal bones and feathers. Around my throat is a necklace made of the skulls of hawks. Their claws pierced through my ears.

My body is brown muscle and scars; for I have battled all my life.

There are five hundred of his mad-eyed priests. There is one of me. What are the odds? Who will the gods gamble on? Roll the die. Place a bet on me.

I have two blades which have been blessed in the Temple of Moons. They curve, decapitate heads easily. I prayed in that temple; I knelt on the stone floors. "Make me a weapon," I said.

Zap!

The gods answered with a lightning bolt. Struck me down.

I woke... dragonflies dancing in my head on the temple floor. The butterfly tattoo on my back was moving, shifting under my skin. Its wings were beating.

I spun, my blades in my hand. They whirred like a hummingbird. Fast as magic. I pounded my foot on the temple floor. A crack appeared, zigzagging. Wobbling the temple pillars.

POWER.

What does it feel like?

There are five hundred of them. There is one of me. Pity them.

I walk through the valley to the Temple of Butterflies. The sun above me frazzles, bounces off the earth.

Those five hundred black-robed priests bow down before the mad sorcerer. Chanting, swaying; saliva drips from their tongues. Fever hot. Devil roast. Watch them move like waves of black water. Surround him in worship. Drown him in it. Under their robes, the flash of a silver dagger; under their smiles, a beautiful nothing.

The Magician holds an ebony staff; he sits on a throne of skulls overlooking his world. I hope the skull of my ancestor bites his bottom.

Butterflies are painted throughout his temple, dazzling from top to toe. A shimmer of wings in every shade of magic.

The gods peer down from their heavens. I am within their theatre. I am part of the entertainment.

I raise my blades. I shout, "MY NAME IS IZEL AND I WILL AVENGE MY PEOPLE, DEMON SORCERER!"

The Magician rises from his throne, his butterfly

mask glints eye-blinding gold. Wet tongued, his acolytes turn their heads and examine me. Googly eyes, demented.

The Magician laughs at me. That's his first mistake.

I shout, "YOUR HEADS ARE MINE!"

I run into his acolytes, the black-mass of them. I chop them into pieces. I am twice the height of most of them, crush one under my foot, pull a head off another. Kick one up the backside – they fly half a mile into the distance.

Easy peasy.

I pick up an acolyte and throw him across the temple as if he were a pebble. I grab another by his legs and spin him round, screaming. Turn him into a whirlwind.

One by one, I end them.

Heads are flying off, bouncing down the steps. They circle me in their black robes, try to fold me into their space.

I make them into a massacre. Chop chop chop chOP chOP CHOP CHOP CHOP CHOP!

Up the steps I climb; a river of blood flows. Behind me a mountain of body parts.

At the top, sizzling gold, the demon Magician waits for me on his throne of skulls, amused by the spectacle.

He squirms, considers me for a moment. "Perhaps we could come to some sort of arrangement?"

I am saturated in blood. It has become my skin. I have no more words for him.

He raises his staff and casts a bolt of black lightning at me which fizzes and crackles. Achieves nothing.

"Stupid bloody thing!" He curses his staff and tosses it down the steps of his temple.

What is that I can smell? Under the mask I smell fear. Under the mask I smell shit and the stink of cowardice. Under the mask I smell *you*, little sorcerer.

I decapitate him in one swoop of my blades; hold his head aloft to the gods and then boot it into the air. It frazzles up in the sunset.

I sit on the throne of skulls, on the heads of my grandfathers. I use the headless corpse of the Magician as a cushion for my feet.

PART ONE

I am Zedock Heap.

The prime minister of England.

A cannibal.

A killer of women and, of course

A DEMONIC MULTI-TASKER.

I gaze at your little London. The vein of the Thames throbs. The ooze glistens. Is that a bloated corpse floating past? Beauty they say is in the eye of the beholder.

SO BEHOLD!

What beauty is this! What filth, what wondrous sludgy intestines. Underneath you are blood-works, pus and a slippery quivering squash of brain.

17

Wretched amusing creatures you are: flopping, eaters of shit. Criminally incompetent. Turds in top hats. How you ever survived this long is beyond all reason. Beyond all stars.

London, London, London. I hold your heart in my hands, my love.

I SQUEEZE YOU.

The framed picture of a map of London explodes behind me under the pressure of my love. Pieces of glass ZOOM through the air: impale the wallpaper.

I'm shuffling paperwork on my desk, thumbing through a catalogue on dungeon equipment. *Sigh.* Aha! A spiked Iron Maiden, a horse whip with an electrical current running through it (how inventive!). And on the very last page, my favourite, a simple garrotte. Slice a salami with it. A foot, perhaps?

TORTURE EQUIPMENT. TORTURE EQUIPMENT. Torture equipment. TORTURE equipment. SAY IT IN AS MANY WAYS AS YOU WANT. It always boils down to the same thing.

You invented it.

You make me smile and you make me so very, very sad.

What use is there for devils like me, when you are so keen to DISSECT one another?

HELL is under your feet. It has always been under your toes.

Oh! A knock at my door, and it creaks open. An eyeball peers through; a nervous shuffle.

"Ah, Mr Evening-Star. Do come in."

He enters smiling nervously, "Morning, Prime Minister."

I close the catalogue of torture equipment. Shut the lid on your toy box. "How can I assist you?"

"Erm, well it's about tonight's *preparations*."

"Yes?" and I lean back in my chair and put my feet up on the desk. I'm a big man. My feet dangle off the end, knock off the paperweight. Mr Evening-Star throws himself to the floor to retrieve it.

I can't conceal my smile, it spreads. Reveals teeth.

He puts the paperweight back on the desk, restores the balance within the world. "We have a little problem," he squeaks.

"Which is?" and I stare into him. Apply pressure to his ribcage.

He trembles. Forces the air out, squeezes out the words, "Please... stop."

He falls to his knees. I'm fascinated by the noises

he makes, the possibility of a *crunch*.

The violence in me bubbles; it is a form of weird alchemy. If you peel the skin off me I am a landscape of hell underneath. I WOULD MAKE YOU MELT INTO ME. I WOULD INGEST YOU into my terrain. Come, put your finger in my mouth; feel the sizzle. Feel things from my point of view. Take a vacation. CROSS OVER THE LINE INTO ME.

I let him go; he collapses to the carpet on his knees. Shuddering, he finally stands back up, adjusts his spectacles.

"Get to the point, Mr Evening-Star; I am, after all, a very busy man. I have an appointment with the Queen later and if you think I'm a challenging employer, SHE WOULD REALLY UNHINGE YOU."

"The women," he stutters, "One of the women escaped, jumped out of the window."

"That is unfortunate," I sigh. "Those cages really aren't up to much are they?"

"No," he agrees and shuffles backwards a little. Subconsciously. It's quite endearing really. "I... I could speak to a welder?"

I burst out laughing and take my feet off the desk, stand up and pat him on the shoulders.

He actually squeaks, flinching violently. Mutters, "It was only the one, I will make sure it doesn't happen again, sir. We have plenty of them for you to... eat." His lips quickly press into a submissive line.

I pluck my hat and coat which hang on a hook by the door. Liquorice-black fur and top hat with a silver sash. I gaze at myself in the looking glass while he fumbles nervously behind me,

I am **magnificent** to look at.

The mirror cracks down the middle. Makes me a zig-zag.

Meanwhile...
MR LOVEHEART TAKES A STROLL
BY THE THAMES

It is a day of custard! It wobbles!

Today I wear electrical blue (I sizzle!). My trademark hearts are splattered up the sides; they ooze into the fabric. I am also sporting a rather fetching set of thigh boots. I like to strut long the path, twiddle my ancestral sword and then LEAP! and hide behind a bush: JUMP! out on random strangers! HA HA! ha ha ha

It is so funny!

An old man screams! His eyes of jelly wibble and quiver.

I have come into London for a spot of cake. I was getting bored at home and I have no servants to talk to. I found one of them dead near the pond, half-eaten. I was quite unnerved and had a conversation with the remaining lower half of the corpse and, of course, apologised profusely for his being eaten and in my garden no less! And so, I am quite alone and I feel unable to employ the lower half of a torso as a butler, as it would perhaps not be altogether practical. He would have considerable problems boiling an egg and roasting a crumpet over the fire (being dead and having no arms, he having being consumed by something as yet unidentified).

The Thames is a fat ooze. Greenish slop waters, occasionally pulling with it dead bodies, purple with bloat. And eels! See them wriggle and flop; see them slither!

London, you are a City of the Dead. Creatures hop and scuttle; jump out their graves; dance over black waters.

If I dip my hands into the Thames, my skin would prickle under the slime water. It would shrivel; feel globular vegetation; growths of slithery lumps.

London, London (and I twiddle my sword in a loop), London, London, London, You are an EATER of the dead. CHOMP CHOMP CHOMP. How unique you are; how horrible! how dazzling! Show me your teeth: expose your tongue to me. UNROLL YOURSELF.

I dance! I dance along the path. Do I hear music?

I strike a pose! Spear a clergyman's hat. Hold it aloft. He screams and crosses himself. Becomes hysterical. I enquire where I might find an excellent piece of cake and after he has recovered his senses (and his hat) he points me in another direction. MAKES ME TURN.

Oh, London, your foul underwater botanical gardens are charming. Bruised purples, blubbery greens, violent turquoise, acidic yellow swirls. Vivid and slimy. Let me count the insects that hum over you. The low buzz of your tiny messengers; the shimmer of their wings.

ANGELS! THEY ARE YOUR ANGELS!

A pigeon lands on my head!

I strut along the path. Twirl. Shoot my pistol in the air. BANG!

The naughty pigeon flies off, craps on the clergyman.

I walk the path. Big Ben strikes. Moves us forward. Time, time, time, you are malleable, misunderstood.

BANG! (I shoot my pistol again.)

I see a fiddler ahead, bashing out a tune near a bench. He taps his spindly leg, plucks a string. It snaps! Thwacks him in the forehead. I hear his swear words on the air: "You f— b—!" he screams. Marvellous!

Heaps of plum coloured clouds swirl above me: marshmallow soft. Hot chocolate! I hear the clanging of bells sound from the church. I raise my head, spy a raven, a gloomy thing glaring at me from a rooftop. Small plucky blue flowers sprout near my feet. Am I a toadstool? A magic mushroom perhaps?

The air whiffs of bubbling jam. I am hungry. I can think of nothing but pudding! I think of custard, cream and the goo of melted chocolate. My mind wanders to jelly beans and strawberry tarts. My stomach rumbles. I flash a smile at an old lady in a bonnet. I bow very low. "Madam, could you direct me to an interesting bit of sponge?"

She bashes me over the head with her umbrella.

"Thank you, my good woman!" I reply. Composing myself and straightening my beautiful coat I head along the path towards the fiddler. I smell fish bones, sea snails, lobster pots, eel pie and mash. A spot of gravy! A splat of mushy peas.

I shout out to the Raven, "WHERE IS THE STRAWBERRY TART, YOU VILLAIN?!"

He caws back at me rather sarcastically.

I spin my ancestral sword and approach the fiddler. He eyeballs me with… is that some sort of suspicion?

"Good morning!" I say

"Got a penny for me to pluck a tune, sir?" he replies grinning with his remaining teeth.

I fling him some paper money in his upside down battered top hat.

"Blimey," he says, staring inside the hat,

"Do you know the tune 'Boil Him in the Pot'?" I ask.

"No, sir, but for this amount of money I can make it up as I go along!" and he picks up his fiddle.

"Wonderful," I reply and lean on my sword, glance at the copious amount of weed life that blooms near the wall.

His fiddle creates music no sane mind could cope with. A screech and twang from the very depths of Hell.

I hum along, go mad with it. The fiddler clicks his tongue, screams out the tune. A brick soars through the air! Hits him between the eyes. GOOD GRIEF! He falls backwards. Perhaps dead!

I spin! Look for the person responsible. Hear laughter. See a pair of eyes peer over the wall. A street urchin sticks out his tongue and runs off over a graveyard, leaps over the dead, out of this world.

I keep moving, wave goodbye to the river, to the ooze. I pluck a windfall apple, squeeze it in the palm of my hand, as though a human sacrifice. I pick up the pace, move faster.

Oh day of custard. Take me to your tearooms. SHOW ME YOUR CAKE!

I am rather lonely. Yes, lonely. LOnEly. LoNelY. Lonely. LOnely. LONELY. Odd word, that.

I am lonely.

Lonelylonelylonelylonelylonelylonelylonelylonely lonelylonelylonelylonely lonelylonelylonelylonely lonelylonelylonelylonelylonely.

What does it mean to be this way?

What flavour ice cream am I inside? SCOOP ME OUT & FIND OUT!

I prod my lacy cuffs. Wave at a ghoulish nanny with a squeaky pram. She shrieks, goes faster. Does she hear music too? I wave goodbye to the nanny and the pram. Wave at the pigeon. Wave at the gloomy raven. I have no one to play with.

My only servant is dead: half-eaten, lying on my lawn. I must remind myself to get him buried, perhaps near the deformed cucumbers near the pond.

I peer across at the Houses of Parliament where my father gave speeches. Monocle wobble and click of silver cane. Lord Loveheart.

DADDY DADDY DADDY.

And now that is my name. I have taken letters, become meaning. Inherited words. Daddy.

I am the richest man in England. I am a Prince of the Underworld and yet, I am only a series of letters. Rearrange me and make some other word.

Invisible music moves me forward.

If you cut open my brain, what would you find, I wonder?

Am I made of jelly? CAN YOU MAKE ME WOBBLE?

I feel the underneath. I feel London's layers. The hot, hot, hot. The sizzle red. Underneath your footsteps are dinosaurs. Fossils of monsters; ribcages of man eaters. Strange spiral shells, deformed looking rocks, horned pieces of another species. The imprint of monsters. MAN-EATER, MAN-EATER, MAN-EATER

I cut the air with my sword.

"Beware what is underneath!" I shout to nothing and no one.

We are
       sinking
              below.

DARWINISM

Evolution theory

COMPETE, SURVIVE AND REPRODUCE
Or, become finger food.

I walk the path; I walk the dark coils of London, her black ribbon entrails. I move into her stomach. It's surprisingly warm here.

The tearooms appear! Manifest before me. A pot of tea and an enormous slab of chocolate cake will be mine, for I am a Prince of the Underworld, and I do love a moist piece of cake.

My loneliness, the empty space inside me needs something to fill it. Squeeze out the air. Over-eat. Feed myself love. Replace kisses with sugar.

Mr Loveheart & Mr Zedock Heap
MEET BY COINCIDENCE AT THE
STUFFED FIG TEAROOMS

The moon is a lollipop. I hold it on a stick. Lickety split. It tastes like pieces of me.

I am sitting by the window of the Stuffed Fig tearooms, an enchanting hovel near London Bridge. Low ceilings, unstable foundations, could quite possibly collapse at any moment. How exciting! I am informed it is also a magnet for poets and authors of the macabre, for the property is apparently haunted. Built on a plague pit. Isn't that wonderful? So much character. Ghost hunters have been rumoured to frequent this establishment in search of evidence of life beyond death. My own suggestion, if you're seeking such evidence, is that you need look no further than to sample the homemade cakes.

I prod my slice of chocolate fudge cake. I slam it

against the wall. It makes a dent in the brickwork. This fudge cake is not of this world.

"What black magic is this?" I say with glee.

The patisserie chef, a meat-faced wall of muscle, emerges from the kitchen. "Is there a problem?"

"This cake is remarkable! It should be worshipped as an ancient god. It will not yield!" I slam it against the table and it bounces off, undamaged.

"Are you taking the piss?" His heavyset lower jaw crunches into a line.

"No. I am expressing delight. It's not really a cake. It's almost, dare I say, A BRICK! You could build a pagan temple with this and it would withstand the lightning strikes of the gods," I cry aloud. The customers look a bit nervous. Why is that, I wonder?

"I think he's saying it's a bit dry," coughs a little bespectacled man in the corner.

The chef removes a cleaver from his apron. "Well, well. We've got a comedian."

"Sir, may I enquire what a pastry chef is doing wielding a meat cleaver? Is this not a tearooms?" I ask, examining a sugar lump to see if it too holds occult powers.

Ting-a-ling! The bell above the tearoom door rings and a tall gentleman in a very stylish top hat and long coat steps in. MMMMmmmmmm, he looks like a demon to me.

The chef hides his meat cleaver, smiles politely at the gentleman and shouts, "Emma?"

Emma appears, short, grinning, face like a happy dumpling. "Yes?"

"Take the prime minister's order."

"Oh, hello, Mr Heap," she curtsies.

"Coffee and a pot of cream," he purrs.

"Very good, sir," and she hurries off.

I approach his table. "If I may warn you, sir, against sampling the chocolate slab."

Mr Heap raises his eyes. "And you are, sir?"

"Interested in what you are."

He smiles. I've seen that sort of smile before. It's power. It's ancient. It's trouble. It's something from underneath.

I tap my sword against the table leg.

"Young man, don't play games with me." His voice suddenly changes tone, deadly serious. **"Because you will regret it."** His eyes fizzle with tiny white explosions.

Oooh, he is a predator!

I twiddle my sword and bow. "My name is John Loveheart and I'm a prince of the Underworld. I also happen to know that this cake," (my sword prods the chocolate slab), "is the most frightening thing I have ever happened across. It's quite unsettled me."

Mr Heap stands up, the chair creaking, and stares into me. Oooooohhhh! The walls of the Stuffed Fig are closing in; he's putting pressure on the structure. What sort of demon is he?

Two customers eating scones and jam in the corner suddenly explode over the walls.

"BACK OFF!" he says and holds me by the throat. My legs dangle in the air. He looks into me, deep underneath the layers of frill and growls, "You're quite mad," and he seems pleased. The windows explode; the walls compress. His eyes hold pieces of an exploding star. And then he laughs, "Little mad prince, that is what you are. Hearts in your eyes. No match for me," and flings me against the wall. I bounce off it and land gracefully on my feet, then unfortunately slip on a slice of lemon tart and slide along the floor into the cake stand.

"That's just bad manners," the remaining survivor of the clientele in the corner says, a slice of fig tart in his hand. "Flinging people against walls."

The demon clicks his fingers and the gentleman explodes.

The chef appears with the cleaver, "Is everything satisfactory?" followed by "Oh fucking hell" and disappears with the speed of a rat up a drainpipe.

I take out my pistol and shoot the demon in the backside. He is not impressed and grabs hold of me by my waistcoat and holds me up in the air and screams, "I AM FROM THE BOWELS OF HELL, LITTLE PRINCE. I AM THE STUFF OF NIGHTMARES."

The building starts to collapse and he folds his furry coat over me and we disappear as the ceiling falls.

Fizz-bang-WHOOOOOOOSH!!

We reappear inside a pagan temple of blood-soaked walls. How thrilling!

He's sitting on a throne of skulls and I... I am rather unfortunately inside a cage that appears to be constructed of human bones, with an intricate human-finger lock mechanism. I can smell fireworks and glitter, and I can hear screaming and some sort of sinister gurgling. Perhaps the drains need unblocking?

"This isn't very sporting," I cry, and I shoot the lock. The bullet sadly bounces off and pings against the wall, followed by a series of pings as it ricochets in several directions and finally lodges itself in a pot plant.

"You are an infuriation, Mr Loveheart," he sighs, staring at me with laser intensity from his throne, "and I will teach you a lesson in manners."

"How did you get voted in?" I twiddle my sword

"I ATE the competition. Now you will learn humility and respect for your elders."

The world around me turns into space. Stars wink, crash and tumble. I am surrounded by indigo night space, and my father's body floats past me. Dead thing in space amongst asteroids and pieces of fizz and spin.

Daddy. Daddy. Daddy. I reach out and try to touch him, but he drifts past me, moves on. It is just an illusion and yet my heart is breaking. Tears wet my face.

Stars fade, the curtain drops.

"You're all alone," he says from his throne, his voice a hypnotism. "Everything you love is dead. It has disappeared. Turned into stardust. Little Prince, insignificant... insane," and he chuckles.

Under the pain, under the breaking in me, there is something turning. Some change. A form of rage. It blooms gigantic petals, unfurls like a flower.

I stand up in the cage, grip my ancestral sword. "I am a prince of the Underworld and you will have to do better than that!"

He leans forward on his throne of skulls, "If you cross my path again, interfere again, I will EAT you."

He clicks his fingers.

I am with the pigeon by the Thames. I am out of reach.

It is four-thirty in the afternoon. A time for buttered teacakes with a splodge of jam.

My name is Pedrock Frogwish and I am ten years old. I am with my little sister Boo Boo, who is six, and we are sitting in a train carriage accompanied by the Reverend Plum, who sits by the window absorbed in a novel entitled *A Dangerous Romance on the Moors*. He licks his long agile fingers as he turns the pages; the wet sound has become increasingly annoying since we left King's Cross Station. He is accompanying us to our Uncle's house in the village of Darkwound, on the outskirts of London, for Boo Boo and I are orphans. We are essentially unwanted. We have been staying for the last two years in the convent of Saint Thomas near Charing Cross, full of kind, well-meaning nuns. Reverend

Plum has made it his mission to find our relatives who now, I suppose, have reluctantly agreed to house us.

I know Boo Boo will miss Sister Martha, who was her favourite nun. Sister Martha had a fascination with dinosaurs and would draw the beasts, scissor-toothed and fat-tailed on the blackboard, and the words *EAT OR BE EATEN*. Words which were scrubbed off by Sister Harriet, who said that there were no such things as dinosaurs and God certainly wouldn't have created such monstrosities. I smile at my sister, who is squeezing her frog puppet toy lovingly around the neck.

She shouts at me: "EAT OR BE EATEN! EAT OR BE EATEN! EAT OR BE EATEN!"

The Reverend Plum looks up from his well-thumbed novel. "Boo Boo, please be quiet."

Boo Boo and the frog puppet stare defiantly back while the Reverend returns to *A Dangerous Romance on the Moors*.

"Is it an absorbing read?" I ask.

Reverend Plum, annoyed, glances up from his forbidden treat. "Yes, it's an enjoyable distraction."

"What's the story about?"

He looks uncomfortable. "Well. It's a love story."

"Between who?"

"Between a priest and a," (he pauses) "farm girl. It's actually more of a warm friendship."

"Warm friendship?"

Boo Boo interrupts his answer "I AM A DINOSAUR! I AM A DINOSAUR AND I AM GOING TO EAT YOU!"

The agitated Reverend Plum, desperate to get back his book, raises his hands in the air. "Boo Boo, shut up! Pedrock, find something to occupy yourself with." And he settles back into the pages of the lusty moors.

I ruffle my sister's hair and the frog puppet stares back at me with an open mouth.

"I love you," I say to Boo Boo.

The frog puppet replies, "I love you, too," and plants a kiss on my cheek.

The train chugs gently onwards through the countryside. It is a wonderful summer's day. Peach coloured sky and soft ice-cream clouds hang over wild flower meadows and forests full of fairy tales. I wonder what our new lives will be like. Will we be loved? Boo Boo doesn't remember our parents, but I do. I remember their faces and the colour of their eyes, which were gingerbread brown. I remember that our Daddy had a little sailing boat, which he took me on once in a moat full of water flowers. The sail was goblin green. We pretended we were pirates. We pretended we were anybody but ourselves.

I hold Boo Boo's hand. I tell her we shall be safe, we shall be loved. I tell her there are fairies in the woods; they live inside trees and eat flowers. They will protect her, draw magic circles around her; sprinkle her with stardust. Make her one of them.

"What about Froggy" she says. "Will they make him a fairy?"

"No, they'll make him a prince with his own kingdom."

This makes her happy. I wish I could give her something other than words.

We are pulling into the station now, for Darkwound. The paint is flaking off the sign like skin. Reverend Plum gathers his bags together and takes Boo Boo's hand.

"Come along children."

We follow him out of the carriage and onto the platform. Somehow the earth beneath my feet doesn't seem solid enough, as though it's about to give way. I am sinking into an unknown space.

Happy birthday to me. Happy birthday to me! HAPPY BIRTHDAY, MR LOVEHEART, happy birthday to me!

I'm having a party today in the gardens of Loveheart Manor, close to the village of Darkwound. I'm eighteen. Mr Fingers, the Lord of the Underworld, is inside a mirror in my hallway, looking rather annoyed. I did offer him a sausage roll from the buffet, but he oddly declined.

It's a glorious hot day of jam. I have prepared everything myself and remembered to bury my half-eaten butler.

Oh joy! We have party food and party guests. I have invited my neighbours, from the village of Darkwound, and they are a surprising bunch. Of course, they have to wear party hats and play games or I'll throw jelly at them. Splatter them with love.

I have heart shaped balloons and decapitated heads hanging from my trees. All local villains of course: a wife beater, a nasty nanny and an author of badly written young adult romance novels. Dingle dangle in the breeze. I put party hats on them; even the dead need some fun.

I've been so lonely since my adventures with Detective White and Walnut. I sent them Christmas presents; some chocolates (laced with a heavy laxative) for Detective White, and a gift wrapped hand grenade for Walnut. I had such fun selecting that.

They sent me a thank you card, of course, which I keep, along with all my correspondence, in the bird cage of the stuffed parrot in the study:

Dear Mr Loveheart,

Words cannot really express my feelings towards your gifts. Thankfully (for me) Walnut ate my chocolates and spent the rest of the day in the Scotland Yard privy. He thanks you for the hand grenade which he keeps in the office, in the biscuit tin.

We hope you received our present, which was a bottle of wild fig brandy.

Kind Regards

   Percival & Walnut

Now where did I put that figgy brandy? Oh, yes, it's in the trifle, under the layer of custard. Soaking up sponge.

Ha ha. Now where was I? Oh yes, Christmas time was very interesting. I had a little adventure involving a zombie Christmas party in Highgate, which I will tell you about on another occasion.

But today is my birthday and I am one year older. One year madder.

The buffet is a dream boat, stuffed with goodies. Ahoy, Captain Sponge Cake! See jellies, green, red and yellow, wobble about merrily. A mountain of whipped cream. Finger food! Sausage rolls and love heart shaped fairy cakes. Heart-shaped balloons float in the air. A giant red heart cake sits in the middle with a devilish cream cheese topping. A splodge of love; dip your finger in and taste the love. Mmmmmm. Custard tarts and a humorous cheeseboard with some dates and a bunch of fat grapes.

Let me introduce my party guests. Poking the brie, we have the retired actress and very good friend of mine, Mrs Lavender Charm. She also writes medieval horrors and makes excellent chutney. Her apricot and walnut is my favourite. Her latest book, *Skulls of the Plague Lord*, is marvellous fun. It has people screaming with black pustules, a lot of whipping and sinister limping monks. I've given her a pink party hat; it sits on her head like a fairy crown. Maybe she has a wand in her carpet bag? Make a wish, give her a kiss.

I am wearing, as it's my birthday, my favourite red waistcoat and a red party hat.

"Mr Loveheart," Mrs Charm says, smiling like a good fairy, "don't you look handsome!" and she pinches my cheek. "You lovely naughty boy."

"Sausage roll, my dear lady?" I offer her the plate.

"I can never resist a sausage," she replies, waggling it about.

"Nor should you, Madam," I concur.

The balloons float into the air; see the hearts, see the hearts in my kingdom take flight, float away. Maybe they will find the stars, reach into space. Drift into the cosmos. Become part of a starscape.

I can see you, balloons. I can see you. Off you float, become part of a star map.

Mr Loveheart and his kingdom of hearts.

Let me dazzle you. Fold you into my timelines. Unravel you. Let's go mad together, my love. Juggle teacups. Bend reality like a headmaster's cane. Thwack you on the bottom with it until you understand. I am the magic man and I want to dangle your head from my trees.

See the beautiful balloon go *pop*.

Oh, my mind is wandering again.

Out from the shrubbery steps Rufus Hazard, wearing a wonky orange party hat and smoking an enormous cigar. He's brought his machete with him with which he trims the azaleas.

"Wonderful piece of weaponry this; slices a head off as smooth as butter. I tell you, they just BOING off into the wilderness! Happy Birthday, you mad old fruit," he grins, his red moustache quivering.

"It is marvellous to see you again."

"I never miss a party, old boy. I've just got back from a little excursion in the Highlands. Nearly got sacrificed to a coven of witches. Had to shoot my way out!" He laughs and his moustache wobbles on his upper lip.

"Witches are feisty," I say, biting into a custard tart.

"Indeed they are. One of them had hold of my leg, the saucy mare. I couldn't shake her off. I had to boot her in the head, the minx! Now tell me, who are the other guests, Loveheart? Any beauties for me?"

"Mrs Charm. The retired actress." I point over to the dear lady.

"I saw her as Titania many moons ago. Superb

legs." He sucks on his cigar.

"Lady Beetle and her young son, Horatio." They are loitering by the champagne.

"Fine looking woman. Is she attached?"

"Husband dead. Buried near the compost heap at the back of her estate, so I understand."

"Egads! A black widow spider, eh?" and his eye glitters.

"Mr Grubweed, retired undertaker." He stands alone, spooning an enormous heap of green jelly into a bowl and splatting cream on top.

"Odd-looking fellow. And how do you know these people exactly?"

"It's the first time I've met them, excluding Mrs Charm. They're my neighbours. Aren't they funny."

"Your neighbours? Do you not have any other friends, dear boy?"

"They're all dead or unavailable," I say. "Detective White and Constable Walnut are busy on a case involving a cursed stolen Indian sapphire."

"Sounds familiar," Rufus chortles. "What's the curse?"

"If you touch the jewel you are immediately transported to Aberystwyth."

His cigar falls out of his lips and he shudders. "*Jesus Christ!*" and he whispers low in my ear. "I know a demonologist, a marvellous chap called Professor Toad, who claims that accursed shit hole is a portal to hell."

"Custard tart?" I offer him the plate.

"No, I'm saving my appetite for that vixen, Lady Beetle, and possibly a scotch egg. Now, who is that strange creature?" and he points a finger in the direction of a spindly-looking priest wearing a green party hat and prodding one of the dangling severed heads.

Reverend Wormhole suddenly screams. "OH MY GOD. IT'S REAL. ITS EYEBALL JUST FELL OUT!"

I speak over his screaming. "Reverend Wormhole – he's really very funny. He believes some sort of dark cult is out to assassinate him."

"Really? And why is that?"

"I sneak onto the parish roof at night dressed up in black robes and a pair of horns, and wave through his window."

"Ha ha! You strange banana!" And Rufus slaps me on the back, so my plate of custard tarts wobbles.

Sadly, I am missing a guest. Professor Hummingbird, the eminent collector of butterflies, failed to RSVP. A sure sign that he's suspicious! I will have to pay a little visit to him after the party. Sneak into his gardens. Pluck a daisy or two.

I hand the plate of custard delights to Horatio Beetle, the ghastly spoiled teenage brat.

"I DON'T WANT ANY," he wails.

"Would you mind holding the plate, young man?" I ask.

"NO, BUGGER OFF, YOU WEIRDO," he replies.

"Do you know what happens to boys with bad manners?"

"NOTHING, BECAUSE I'M RICH."

"They explode."

"WHAT?"

"That's right. Suddenly and without warning."

Horatio looks at me with a thick scowl and then takes the plate of tarts.

His mother, Lady Beetle saunters over, "Darling, you're not a servant. Why are you holding that?"

"MR LOVEHEART SAID I WOULD EXPLODE IF I DIDN'T."

I wander back inside Loveheart Manor, take Mr Fingers a piece of the birthday cake. Red and yellow sponge. Tastes like hearts.

"Hello, Mr Fingers, I brought you cake."

He stares at me from his mirror prison like an octopus stuffed in a preservative jar. Eyes full of broken bits and pieces. Discarded. He says nothing, the pickled thing.

Death appears in a fizz-whiff of smoke, wearing a black party hat.

"Happy birthday, Mr Loveheart."

"You certainly know how to make an entrance."

"I brought you a present." He tries to smile, it's very unnerving. And he hands me a box with a big black bow on it.

"I love surprises."

"Well you'll like this then." His expression reveals nothing.

I unwrap it and open the lid. It's a black jewelled crown.

Mr Fingers is screaming, pounding his fists against the mirror.

"Put it on," Death says.

I take off my red party hat. Put the spiked black crown on my head; it glitters of demon magic.

"Your rightful inheritance. You are of age." He nods his head. "Mr Loveheart, Lord of the Underworld."

"NOOOOOOOOOOOOOO NOOOOOOOOOOOO NOOOOOOOOOOO!" Mr Fingers is trying to smash the mirror open.

The crown is very heavy: it feels like the weight of a black star pushing me into the earth. "What does this mean?"

"It means," says Death, helping himself to the birthday cake, "that things are going to get very interesting. There is also an important matter which I need to discuss with you, concerning another gift."

"More presents? How thrilling!"

"Your powers as Lord of the Underworld will now start to manifest and they could come in any form."

"How will I know what they are?"

"I am not sure of the specifics, no one bothers to keep me up to date on these formalities, but it should happen soon."

"That is very exciting news, I wonder what curious powers I will acquire?"

"If you recall, your predecessor, Mr Fingers, had a skill for self-replication to produce heirs."

"Oh yes, they were rather horrible as I recall."

"Yes, well, let's hope you acquire something more useful."

"I can't recall Bad Daddy having any other special powers."

"Well, he had no sense of humour, which is more of a curse," sighed Death wearily, "but he was proficient at manipulation; the gifts vary depending on the individual. And, you know, being Lord of the Underworld makes you exempt from being killed by standard methods."

"Well, that is good news. You won't be sneaking up behind me and hitting me over the head with a lampshade any time soon then? Ha ha."

Death peered over my shoulder, "I would like some more cake please."

"Of course, dear friend, let us go back to the party and cut a hefty slab for you. Oh, and I must tell you before I forget, I met someone rather nasty recently," I say, touching the crown, feeling the zap and tingle.

"Really?" he looks curious.

"Yes, the prime minister."

"VERY careful, Loveheart," said Death, "He's dangerous."

"He rather upset me and I have a mind to have him stuffed and put in the hall."

"Before you strategize your revenge why not enjoy your special day?" He patted me on the back and lead me gently outside the grounds of Loveheart Manor. The sun is sizzling, the fairies are sitting in the trees, laughing, drunk on the trifle. One falls off the branch head first into a rosebush. Splat!

All the roses in my kingdom are red. There's no need for paint.

The crown on my head glints wickedly. Its weight

seems impossible. Death follows me out, under the shadows, and starts chatting to Mr Hazard.

"Have we met?" says Rufus.

"Not yet." His smile is concealed.

I wander deeper into my gardens. These lands stretch on for miles, deep in woods and fields. Cherry and apple trees dangle with fruits. Squashy orbs. See them wibble-wobble and hit the earth. I touch the crown; it zaps my finger. I never saw Mr Fingers wear it. Perhaps he kept it for special occasions. Kept under the sink with the pots of chutney. Well today is special. It is my birthday and I am no longer a mad prince. I am a mad king. But I have no queen to share my kingdom with. No queen

but

so

many

hearts.

Who should I pick? The answer is simple:

SOMEONE
JUST
LIKE
ME.

I sit under the cherry tree with my wicked crown. Perhaps I should advertise in the *Times*?

KING OF the Underworld seeks
Queen. Good sense of humour.
Fond of cakes. Mad as a kilt.
Please apply PO Box…

I eat a cherry, ponder the significance of them as a fruit. Happy Birthday to me. Happy Birthday to me! Happy Birthday to me!

I fall asleep; dream of dark spaces. Untangle myself from a net of the god of sleep. Little fish, little fish. I am in my underworld; the clocks now all move backwards.

I wander inside the dining room of this dark palace; see a coil of intestinal sausage lying on a platter amongst a selection of cut meats. I know I'm dreaming: these are all rooms within my head. This is my kingdom, this is my kingdom. Underneath the world. Underneath the layers; under skin and bone. Curious thing, this crown. It's itching my head. I scratch and look about me at this dream; my underworld. My horror world. Tastes like golden syrup; surprisingly sweet.

I am shaken awake.

"Mr Loveheart?" Mr Hazard grins, big teeth revealed through a fuzz of orange. "Wakey, wakey birthday boy. We're all waiting for the party games."

"Oh how fun!" and I leap to my feet and adjust my crown.

I walk with Rufus back across the garden lawn. The balloons are souls on a string. Someone let go.

I ring a little silver bell, *ding-a-ling*. The eyes of my guest are upon me. "Thank you everyone for coming to my birthday party. It is lovely to finally meet you all. And now I think we shall play a little game of pass the parcel. There's a surprise for whoever wins."

"Mamma," squeals Horatio, "I want the surprise!"

"And if you're lucky," I say darkly, "you shall get it."

(Five minutes later)
OBSERVATION BY MUNGO,
THE GROUNDSMAN OF BEETLE MANOR

I'm leaning on a shovel, observing a suspicious chrysanthemum.

Suddenly I hear an explosion, followed by a scream, and I see young Master Horatio Beetle flying through the air and into the pond. Well, bugger me if I don't race down there as fast as I can and fish the little nipper out.

He's not happy. He tells me to *Sod Off.* I'm tempted to hit him over the head with my shovel but my grandmother taught me good manners, so I help the spoilt rascal back to his mother, who's waiting for him by an overgrown rhododendron bush, holding a heart-shaped balloon.

The black dog

It's a mile walk along a woodland path to our Uncle's house. The Reverend Plum whistles as he walks, gripping Boo Boo's little hand. Her other hand is within the frog puppet, who looks about, googly-eyed in wonder at his surroundings.

"It's simply a glorious day in God's garden," sighs Reverend Plum.

There's a rummaging in the bushes and out steps a young gentleman wearing a purple waistcoat and jacket covered in red hearts. His hair is the colour of angels: a dazzling yellow. In his hands he carries a severed head, whose mutilated stump drips onto the path. He looks at us with his ink black eyes and smiles mischievously. "Good afternoon. I'm afraid if you've come for the party you've missed all the cake!"

Boo Boo is laughing. The reverend screams. The young gentleman keeps walking across the path and into the forest on the other side. The blood trail of the severed head is splattered on the path like rose petals.

"Why does the funny man have a head?" laughs Boo Boo.

"He's a madman! We're all to be murdered!" screams the hysterical Reverend Plum.

"I think we're safe. He's gone," I say.

Reverend Plum makes us run the rest of the way.

My Uncle's house is surrounded by a spiked iron fence and is gloomy looking and run-down. The house is a dirty grey colour with a small herb garden in the back which leads into a tumbling expanse of more woodland. Outside the gates sits an enormous black hound which growls at Reverend Plum.

"My heart can't take much more of this," he says, clutching his chest. Boo Boo lets go of his hand and strokes the dog, who seems very pleased and then rolls over and gets his tummy tickled. I unlock the latch on the gate, which creaks open rather theatrically. The Reverend Plum composes himself and knocks on the door, dizzy with relief.

Walnut and I are on a train pulling out of Aberystwyth station, for the third time. A solitary sheep, who I'm sure recognizes us, stares and bleats, while rain pounds the roof of the train carriage, splattering the windows. The sky is a dismal shade of purgatory-porridge.

Walnut waves at the sheep.

"What did I tell you, Walnut?" I say, exasperated.

"Um…" He stops waving and looks at me shamefacedly. "You said 'Don't touch it or we'll end up in Wales again'."

"*So why did you do it?*"

"I just thought I'd give it a little polish, make it look nice for Inspector Badger."

The curse of this particular jewel transports not only the idiot who touches it but anyone standing

58

within a few feet.

I sink back into my seat. I sigh, exhaling all the air from my lungs. Hopefully, I may pass out. We aren't alone in this embarrassment. Constable Luck and the tea lady, Mrs Sultana, had both been stupid enough to fiddle with that accursed sapphire. Mrs Sultana, having made the most of her surprise day out, had visited her nephew. Apparently he's a locksmith who lives up the road.

"What do you think Chief Inspector Badger will do with the sapphire?" Walnut takes a cheese and pickle sandwich out of his jacket and takes an enthusiastic bite.

"If he has any sense, he'll throw it into the Thames." I look out of the carriage window at the all too familiar swell and dip of vegetable green. The grey drizzle of skyline.

Walnut munches on his sandwich.

The ticket inspector appears with a wide grin. "Well, well," he says, sliding the carriage door open. "You two again. You just can't keep away from our beautiful land." And he starts singing, his eyes glistening over with Welsh mists.

I take my pistol out and aim it at his head. "Stop that at once or I'll shoot you."

Heads on trees
MR LOVEHEART DECAPITATES HIS WICKED NEIGHBOURS

I'm hiding in a bush, observing Fangus Oil, the local drunk who exposes himself to women and random sheep. He's urinating against a tree singing "Scarborough Fair", which alone is an excellent reason for his imminent demise.

I stand behind him and cough politely. "Ahem."

"What do you want?" He turns, peering at me, wobbling, strawberry nosed, smelling like a decomposing corpse.

"My name is John Loveheart and I would like your head. If you would place it in the bag please," and I open the black velvet sack (with trademark love heart) that I've brought with me.

"Are you a little bit funny in the head?" he says, and breaks into song: "Parsleeeey, saaaaage, rosemary and thyme... la la la."

I cut his head off immediately and sling it in the sack.

I creep further into the woods and find Daisy Dungbeetle picking poisonous mushrooms and placing them in her wicker basket. School mistress, avid reader of vampire novels – and part-time murderess.

"Madam," I step out amidst the toadstool ring, "I am here to stop your wicked ways," and I aim my sword at her.

She hisses at me. Bares her teeth, flickers her tongue. Holds a black mushroom up and thrusts it at me. "I curse you with this fungus of the Dark Master."

"Are you threatening me with a mushroom?"

CHOP

I toss her head in the sack.

Lastly, after plucking some wild strawberries from the woodland path, I find Judge Thumpus Zop snoozing in his garden, a copy of the *Times* folded neatly on his lap. He has a reputation for cruelty. I tap his leg with my ancestral sword.

"WHAT THE DEVIL?" he shouts, awakening from his slumber.

"You have been a very bad boy, Judge."

"What are you?"

"The Demon Lord of the Underworld... Ooh, now I've said it aloud it sounds rather impressive."

"Oh crap."

He tries to sprint across the lawn and trips up over a basket of courgettes. Picks one up and tries to stab me with it.

I hang their heads from red ribbons in my gardens. What pretty dingle dangly things. Poke them and they wobble about.

What fun. What fun!

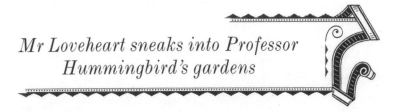

Mr Loveheart sneaks into Professor Hummingbird's gardens

It's a lovely night for a spot of mischief. The cosmos above the little world of Darkwound is soapy; bubbles of star-froth white. Galaxies wink underwater.

The woods around the Professor's moated castle are very thorny. I have already tripped over a warty root and I have had words with it. Given it a good talking to.

His gardens need tending, always a sign of a demented mind. His violets are shrivelled (a sure sign of his unhinged brain) and his water lilies look depressed. Poor things.

I scale the side of his castle, climb up the ivy. Launch myself onto his rooftops and look over his domain. Yes, I think to myself. He's clearly a villain, for I spy weeds sprouting out of his chimney pot.

Mmmmm. I stroll across the roof and find a window open and hang down and peer in. And there he is in his study,

My God!

The wallpaper is hideous. Some sort of floral obscenity!

And his butterflies, hundreds of them framed in glass. Pierced through their hearts.

I smell a killer. What is that he's scribbling? A wicked journal of his atrocities, no doubt.

I lose my footing and fall into the shrubbery below. Whoops! I may have buggered my ankle up.

Leaping out of the bushes I sneak round the garden, observing a very questionable looking potato plant, which I prod with my foot. It explodes in black pus. I need no further proof that he is insane, and cursed with a black finger when it comes to horticulture.

Aha! I find an open window on the ground floor and slip, unnoticed, into his pantry. Mmmmmm is that a pumpkin pie? I am so very fond of pumpkins, they are such an amusing shape.

The pie is excellent. I put my feet up on his kitchen table, eat another slice and contemplate my options.

I wiggle my ankle. Think about stuffing a sock in

his mouth and beating him with his sinister potato plant. Make a mash of him

ya**wn**

I fall asleep, zzzzz Just a little doze. Wake up with a beetroot-faced woman staring at me.

"What the bleedin' hell are you doing in my kitchen?" she yells, her face a bloated thing.

Oops! It's morning.

"Madam," I say, "There's no need to be alarmed, I was just sampling your delicious pumpkin pie."

"Sling yer hook!" and she thwacks me with a tea towel. "GO ON, BUGGER OFF!" and beats me on the bottom with it.

I dart out of the window, shouting, "Farewell, good lady," followed by, "I believe your potato plant may be dead."

She throws a pot at me, which narrowly misses my head and thuds against a tree.

Dinner with the Grubweeds

The dining table sags under the weight of a roast turkey and two roast geese, an enormous mound of roast potatoes, buttered carrots and a pot of steaming gravy. My uncle, Philip Grubweed, sits at the head of the table. He is a retired undertaker who had made a small fortune after a freak outbreak of cholera and with his savings had bought this run - down manor house. He is hugely fat and has several chins which bob up and down, great hairy pink hands and moist piggy little eyes.

"Welcome to your new home, Pedrock and Boo Boo," he says, stuffing a goose leg into his mouth and sucking up the skin.

My Aunt Josephine sits opposite him with a lacy cap perched on her head. She looks half-dead. Skin stretched over her face, gums drawn back, eyes glassy and dull. I think she's hardly aware that we're here. I pass the carrots to her. She ignores me and gazes at the wall.

They have three children sitting round the table. Two girls, Prunella and Estelle, both podgy and blonde, with pink ribbons in their hair, and both aged ten. And a son, who's the eldest at sixteen, called Cornelius. He is stabbing his turkey leg repeatedly with his fork so hard the table shakes.

"Stop that, you little shit!" cries Uncle Grubweed, and belches.

Cornelius mutters something dark under his tongue and puts his fork down begrudgingly.

"We met a most unusual character in the woods today," intervenes Reverend Plum.

"Who?" says Uncle.

"Well, he was dressed most strangely in purple with love hearts, and he was carrying what appeared to be a human head." He laughs, nervously.

"That's one of our neighbours. Mr Loveheart. He's as rich as a prince and as mad as a badger. I was at his birthday party earlier this afternoon. Bizarre affair. Strange puddings!"

"Is he dangerous?" Reverend Plum gulps.

"Well, let's just examine your last statement where you observed he was carrying a human head.

I think you've already answered your own question there, reverend," and my Uncle laughs out loud.

"Would it be possible to have an escort to the station tomorrow morning, just in case he reappears?"

"Cornelius will walk you, won't you son?"

Cornelius is playing with a vein in the turkey leg.

"Excellent. I feel safer already. Do you have any other interesting neighbours, Mr Grubweed?"

Uncle puts his fork down, having skewered a roast potato the size of a fist. "Our nearest is Lady Ursula Beetle and her son, Horatio, who is the same age as Cornelius. He's a handsome devil. Their house overlooks the lake. Deeper in the woods is the home of the retired Professor. He used to teach anthropology or some other nonsense at a university in London. He's an eccentric recluse. And just round the corner in the yellow cottage is the retired actress Mrs Charm. She makes rather nice chutneys."

"Well, I'm sure Pedrock and Boo Boo are going to have lots of fun with all these interesting people," says Reverend Plum, stuffing a buttered carrot into his mouth.

"So, Pedrock," says Mr Grubweed, "do you and your sister have any hobbies?"

"I like sailing, sir."

"Sailing, eh? Well I know Grandpa upstairs has an old boat he might let you use on the lake. And what about you, Miss Boo Boo?"

Boo Boo replies, the frog sock puppet mouthing the answer, "I am a dinosaur. I like to eat people."

"She's a funny little girl. Certainly more lively than my three."

"What about schooling for them?" inquires Reverend Plum.

"Let's not worry about that over dinner. Mrs Charm does some occasional tutoring, I am sure that will suffice. And of course there's Sunday school. The vicar, Mr Wormhole, provides a stimulating environment for young minds."

"It all sounds very encouraging."

The conversation for the rest of the main course comprises of Mr Grubweed going into some length about how you drain a corpse of all its bodily fluids and the price of coffins these days. The pudding is finally brought out: three piping hot apple and blackberry pies with a bowl of hot custard.

I am handed a huge slice, which I drown in custard.

"Who does the big black dog belong to, Mr Grubweed?" I ask.

"He's Grandpa's. His name is Guardian. Tore a man's leg off once, bugger was trying to break into the house."

"How charming. Do you have a local constabulary?" coughs Reverend Plum.

"No. When there's trouble, which there has been, a fella from Scotland Yard pops up and investigates."

"What sort of trouble have you had?"

"Well, apart from the odd thieving and poaching, quite a few people have gone missing over the last few years."

"Missing?"

"Just disappeared. Body parts were found in the woods."

"Good heavens! Has anything happened recently?" asks Reverend Plum.

"Last month, the butcher's wife, Mrs Crumble. They found her foot hanging off a tree on the Beetle estate."

"How did they know the foot was hers?" I ask.

"Clever boy. Well, apparently she only had four toes on one foot. It's probably gypsies, or might be Mr Loveheart having a laugh."

Reverend Plum has gone a peculiar shade of green. "I don't feel very well," he says, putting down his dessert spoon.

"I don't think we can afford to overreact," sighs Mr Grubweed. "There are certain compromises one makes when moving to the countryside."

"Compromises?" cries a flabbergasted reverend.

"There are a lot of weirdoes out here. I'm a man of the world. My own father, who was a bricklayer, used to occasionally dress up in a ball gown and tiara and hang out at the Docks. Body parts in the woods; it's all part of life. I've seen corpses explode before."

"I need to lie down," says Reverend Plum, rising from his chair. "I have a weak heart."

"Josephine will take you to your room." His wife, who hasn't moved all evening, stands very slowly and, lurching like a recently dug up corpse, escorts Reverend Plum into the hallway. I finish my apple pie and have a second helping. It is delicious.

After dinner, Boo Boo and I are taken upstairs to our bedrooms, which are situated in the attic. Boo Boo's is a tiny little room with a small window. I kiss her goodnight and she is tucked in with her frog puppet. Guardian the dog ambles up the stairs and slumps himself outside Boo Boo's bedroom, keeping one eye open.

My own room is larger, with a view overlooking

the herb garden and the woods. I stand on tiptoe and, peering out, can see through the mass of trees a turret peeking through. This, I think, must be the home of the mysterious Professor.

That night I dream the world is made of water. I am on a boat which floats softly on an ocean landscape as blue as angel eyes. A mirror world. I can see fat fish and suffocating vegetation deep underwater, tendrils of black seaweed and mutations of jellyfish. Odd glimpses of scissor-like creatures, horror-white, glistening under the looking-glass ripples.

Bloated egg-laying machines, with rainbow fins, drift lazily by my little boat, which drifts deeper into the water-world. Loosing itself in liquid.

Standing next to me is a man dressed as a police officer, and he puts his hands on my shoulders and whispers in my ear, "They bite."

I wake with a jolt, nearly falling out of bed. I can hear muffled voices from Boo Boo's room.

I put my ear to the wall but I can't make any words out. I get out of bed and step onto the landing where Guardian is sleeping peacefully. I open the door to Boo Boo's room and she is sitting upright in bed. But there is no one else there.

"Are you alright, Boo Boo? I heard voices."

She looks at me curiously. "I had bad dream." She pulls the covers over her head. The frog puppet is sitting on her pillow staring at me.

Mr Loveheart dreams

I lay in a star shape on my giant red four-poster bed, dotted with hearts and big squidgy heart-shaped cushions. I have decided I will get up at lunch time and eat some jam sandwiches.

I snooze, roll over and blot out the slither of sunlight that sizzles through the curtains.

Close my eyes, squeeze them shut. Imagine spaces within spaces. Labyrinths within labyrinths. You go mad inside them. Retrace old footsteps, walk backwards, become part of the hedge. Part of the pattern.

I wink an eye open. See a fat fairy with black wings zoom across the room, hover over my head. She has razor teeth and wings of ebony glitter.

"Oh, hello," I say into the pillow.

She zooms up to my ear, whispers into it. "I have

come to inform you of your Gifts as Lord of the Underworld."

"Excellent, shall we have some jam first."

She slaps me across my cheek and squeaks, "NO, you shall listen to me." Oh, she is rather strict.

She hovers close to my earhole, "Whoever you kiss will live forever and if you kiss the dead they will come back to life."

"Now that is curious."

She continues, this time whispering very low, "You have the gift of madness. You can turn others insane; make their mind turn upside down. The Underworld is also now at your command, my lord."

"That is rather splendid."

Squeak!

Meeting Grandpa Grubweed

Breakfast is enormous, consisting of bacon, eggs, crumpets and honey. It is eight o'clock and I sit in the kitchen with the Reverend Plum, as no one else is out of bed yet. Mrs Treacle, the Cook, pours the tea. She has a kind moon face and gives me a wink.

"Thank you for finding my sister and me a home," I say to Reverend Plum.

"You are very welcome, Pedrock." He butters a crumpet. "I shall be visiting every few weeks to see how you're both doing."

"Are you feeling better this morning?" I enquire.

"Yes, the sleep did me good, although I had the most curious dream."

"Please tell me what it was."

"It was about your sister. She was digging up dead bodies in the garden. Dreams are, of course, caused from lapses of ill health. I believe my intestines have a fungal infection causing me to hallucinate."

Mrs Treacle leans over. "Mr Grubweed wants you to pop upstairs after breakfast and see Grandpa," and she gives me a kiss on the cheek. "I'm making rabbit pie for dinner tonight, and trifle for pudding. Don't worry, Reverend, I've a lunch packed for you for the train. Plenty of ham and cheese sandwiches, and a slab of leftover apple pie."

"Thank you, Mrs Treacle. I look forward to eating them."

After eating far too many crumpets and saying farewell to Reverend Plum, I ascend the staircase and enter Grandpa's room. I find him sitting in an armchair with Boo Boo and Guardian at his feet. He is blind, his eyes white as eggs. He wears a strange Indian green dressing gown and is bald, with a wispy white beard.

"You must be Pedrock." His voice is cool and soothing.

"Yes, sir." I sit by his feet with my sister.

"I was just telling your sister that she's got a friend for life in Guardian. He's an old soppy bugger of a dog and very picky about whom he chooses."

Boo Boo tickles Guardian's nose.

"Now children. You have an adventure ahead of

you today. I want you to visit all your neighbours –
Mrs Charm, Lady Beetle, the Vicar Mr Wormhole,
Mr Loveheart and the Professor. You are to
introduce yourselves. And then you can tell me
what you think of them," he chuckles. "And tonight
my son-in-law informs me that we have a special
guest coming for dinner. His name is Icarus
Hookeye, he's a friend of the Professor. Isn't that
exciting! Now, off you go and have some fun. And
Pedrock…"

"Yes, sir?"

"I shall arrange for you to take my boat out.
Would you like that?"

"Yes, sir, very much, thank you."

And we leave him dozing off in his chair and
begin the lakeside trudge into the village. Mrs
Treacle has made Boo Boo a bacon sandwich and
one for Guardian, the smell enchanting the air like
a wicked spell.

The path to the village trickles round the edge of
the lake which is flat and calm with mottled
feathered ducks floating aimlessly on its surface.
Butterflies with fairy-glamour wings of cotton white
and fizzy pink hang in the air, skimming over the
toady water-reeds and lumpish rocks.

The village itself is very small and consists of a pub

called The Highwayman, a butcher's, apothecary, bakery and church. We agree our first call should be to see Mr Wormhole, the vicar.

The church is small and medieval with a tiny graveyard filled with dandelions. We find Mr Wormhole kicking a crumbling gravestone with his foot, shouting, "Bloody thing!"

"Hello," I say.

"Oh, I do apologise." He looks up at us. "I keep tripping over this thing. I nearly twisted my ankle."

"We are living with our Uncle Grubweed. My name is Pedrock and this is my sister Boo Boo."

He casts a beady eye over us. "I hope I shall be seeing you both every Sunday. We could do with some new blood in this community. People keep going missing," and he looked suspiciously over his shoulder. He has the most shocking messy red hair and great bushy red eyebrows.

"We were previously staying in a convent near Charing Cross."

"An excellent beginning to life." He waggles a finger at the dandelions. "I, too, was raised by nuns. My mother left me in a bucket outside St Ursula's Convent."

"I'm so sorry to hear that."

"Oh no, young Pedrock. It was a gift. I was

educated, well fed and loved. Nothing more a child requires." He walked with us down the path towards the church. "If it had not been for those nuns, I would not have found the joy of God." He slips on a ropey-looking weed and falls face forward into an open grave. After helping pulling him out, we say our farewells.

Our next stop is Mrs Charm's cottage, which is on the edge of the village, near the bakery. The cottage is lemon yellow and her garden is covered in lavender. I knock furtively on the door and a very short lady with a mane of grey curly hair which falls down to her waist greets us. She has lavender entwined in her braids and her eyes are sparkling, grey and mischievous.

"Good morning," she says.

I introduce us.

"Ahhhh... three scallywags. Do come in. I have a pot of tea and some fruitcake."

The cottage has very low ceilings and is stuffed full of herbs, with little pots filled with jam and pickles. On her stove a large pot is bubbling, a sweet smelling concoction. We sit round the table, Guardian slumping on the rug by Boo Boo's feet.

"My Uncle says you are a retired actress."

"That's correct, dear. Now I focus my attentions

on writing novels," and she generously cuts the fruit cake into great slabs and puts them on plates in front of us.

"What sort of novels?" I ask.

"Horror, mainly," and she smiles. "I am currently writing a medieval saga set in a haunted monastery. My hero, a young monk named Maximilian, is subjected to the most vivid nightmares, and then, becoming possessed by a demonic force, murders everyone in a five mile radius."

"It sounds very interesting. Have you ever read *A Dangerous Romance on the Moors*? Our acquaintance, the Reverend Plum, was very taken with it."

"I can't say that I've heard of it," she says, thinking to herself. She throws a piece of cake to the dog, who sniffs it, and then devours it avidly. "This is actually my first Medieval Horror Saga novel. I hope to complete a series of them." Her eyes wander to her shelf of colourful preserves. "You must take some of my new batch of nettle and tomato chutney. It has hints of rosemary in it for protection against malicious gossip." She rises from her chair and starts to pour some of the gloopy constituents into a couple of jam jars, and then, twining a green ribbon into a bow round each of them, hands them to me.

"There you go, Pedrock."

"Thank you, Mrs Charm. We are to visit Lady Beetle, Mr Loveheart and the Professor."

"Mr Loveheart often drops in for a literary discussion. He is very fond of books and of my raspberry jam. Lovely man, with a theatrical dress sense. I am very fond of him. As for Mrs Beetle and her son Horatio, I've only met them a couple of times. Not chutney lovers. But polite enough. The Professor I have only heard of by reputation; he's said to have a brilliant mind and has become a recluse. He's obsessed with the Aztecs, you know."

"Sister Martha at the convent told us about the Aztecs. She said they performed human sacrifices and ate hearts."

Boo Boo shouts, "I want to eat a heart."

"Indeed?" Mrs Charm raises an eyebrow.

"We have already met Mr Wormhole, and he seemed rather distracted."

"Yes, poor fellow, I am sure that some great tragedy has befallen him in the past. Or perhaps some misalignment with the hemispheres of the brain. His sermons are notoriously appalling. I have been trying to help him with his stage presence and speech deliverance."

We stay with her for an hour and she tells us

about her life as a Shakespearean actress in London. Her most memorable role was as Queen Titania playing opposite a drunk Oberon who fell off the stage and was carried back on by the fairies. Improvisation, she says, is the key to great acting.

We wave goodbye and make our way along the long winding path to the Beetle Estate, the bees swarming over a great heap of crimson roses that grow in a mass by the lakeside. Boo Boo tries to pull some out and cuts her hands on the thorns, examining the blood curiously and then licking it. There is a rustling from the bushes, the roses waggle about and Mr Loveheart appears, grinning, thankfully not holding a head. He is dressed this time in peacock blue. His hair is sticking up on end rather messily.

"Hello again. We haven't been properly introduced. I am Mr Loveheart," he says.

"My name is Pedrock and this is my sister Boo Boo."

Boo Boo steps forward and shakes his hand. "You are the funny man with the head."

"Yes, I am," and he bows very low, winking at my sister. Then we hear a shotgun go off and men shouting, "COME BACK HERE, YOU LUNATIC!"

"If you'll excuse me, some locals are trying to

shoot me," and he scampers off back into the bushes.

"Goodbye. Nice to have met you," I call out.

"I like him," says Boo Boo.

The Beetle residence is a grand, cream-coloured house with a very tidy lawn that stretches to the rim of the lake. It is serene, if a little characterless. The manservant escorts us to the garden where Lady Beetle sits under a large, pink, lacy parasol, writing what appear to be invitations. The manservant introduces us and Lady Beetle looks up from under her parasol, inspecting us. She has dark little eyes and is quite pretty. She hands me an envelope.

"Please give this to your Uncle. We're having a little party next Saturday. It saves me the trouble of posting it."

Guardian the dog cocks a leg at the back of her chair. Mercifully she doesn't see him.

"Thank you," I respond, keeping a firm eye on Guardian.

She seems a little inconvenienced at our presence and sighs rather affectedly. "I am rather busy today, children, and my son Horatio has been sent to Cambridge to visit my sister. He will be back for the party and I am sure you will meet him then." She turns her eyes away from us and continues writing her invitations. "I am sure," she says without glancing at us, "that you can see yourselves out."

And so we do.

The walk to the Professor's house is through deep woods, the light from the sun almost blanketed by the thickness of the trees which cover our heads. The air is cool and eerie. Guardian chases a rabbit through the undergrowth, wagging his tail happily. Boo Boo picks forget-me-nots and makes a chain and puts them wonky in her hair. Finally, we come upon the house, which is a crumbling medieval keep with a tower, surrounded by a moat with a little wooden bridge.

"The wizard lives here," says Boo Boo. She points a finger at the tower.

We cross the bridge and walk into a courtyard where a gentleman with white hair and gloves stands. He is pacing up and down, smoking a pipe. Seeing us, he stops suddenly and moves towards us. "Can I help you?"

Guardian growls softly and places himself in front of Boo Boo.

"Are you the Professor?" I ask.

"No, I am an associate of his. My name is Icarus Hookeye. And your dog doesn't seem to like me very much."

"Oh. I think you are having dinner with my Uncle tonight."

"Grubweed? Yes, I have some business with him."

He eyes me coolly.

"We have come to introduce ourselves to the Professor."

"It won't be possible to see him today. As you can see, I have been waiting for some time."

He sounds irritated.

I don't know what else to say to him so we leave and he watches us go. As we cross the bridge Boo Boo points again at the tower and I see the face of a man peering down at us from the upper most window, partially obscured by shadow.

The forest vegetation is thick about our ankles, suffocating the sunlight. Custard yellow toadstools ripen amidst a mass of furry, greenish moss. Creepy crawlies spy on us from the knots in trees, those hidden and secret spaces. Watching us, antennas twitching.

We are under insect surveillance.

Icarus Hookeye comes for dinner

When Icarus Hookeye arrives, the moon has risen and is hanging like a mirror in the black velvet of the night sky. Uncle Philip greets him with a firm handshake and escorts him into the dining room where Mrs Treacle's rabbit pies sit steaming alongside heaps of buttered mash potatoes and a shredded cabbage.

"First dinner, and then business," says Uncle Grubweed. He spoons an excessively generous portion of mash onto his plate while Sally the maid pours red wine into the gentlemen's glasses.

"And where is Mrs Grubweed?" enquires Mr Hookeye.

"She is feeling a little frail this evening and keeping her father company upstairs. It is no particular loss, she is a woman of very few words."

That's an understatement, I think.

Cornelius is kicking the leg of Prunella's chair.

"Daddy, tell Cornelius to stop!"

Uncle Philip stands up and smacks Cornelius round the back of the head so hard his head falls forward into his dinner. Prunella and Estelle are laughing. Cornelius runs out of the room, covering his face.

I am sat next to Mr Hookeye. I notice he has turquoise eyes which remind me of coloured glass, as though he were a character in a stained glass window.

"I am quite glad I have never had children," he says, looking directly at me.

Mr Grubweed replies, "Mine are little brats. I am hoping to get these two," (pointing to Prunella and Estelle) "married off in the next few years. Horatio Beetle will do very nicely as a son-in-law. We Grubweeds may not have an illustrious ancestry, but we've got money. Lady Beetle can't turn her nose up at that."

"Do you teach at the university?" I ask Mr Hookeye.

"No. I am a doctor. I am the Professor's personal physician."

"How is the old fart?" Uncle says.

"In a foul mood, it seems." He gives my Uncle a knowing glance.

"Well, I'm sure his mood will pick up within time."

"It had better," Hookeye says, glaring disapprovingly at the cabbage on his plate.

The conversation over dinner goes into some length over Lady Beetle and her son, Horatio. Lady Beetle is a widow whose husband died of a stroke a few years ago. My Uncle describes her as a handsome but cold woman and Horatio as the "prize". He is looking forward to the party at the Beetle mansion, where he can show his daughters off.

When pudding arrives, Mr Hookeye is already looking bored and declines and so my Uncle takes him into the study to discuss business. We children are left with the towering trifle. Boo Boo eats only the custard layer and feeds the sponge to the dog. I very much want to listen to what Uncle and Mr Hookeye are saying and so excuse myself and put my ear to the study door which is slightly ajar. They are arguing about something I can't make out. The Professor is angry with them both for something. Uncle shouts, "That old devil, he'll drag us both to hell!" and then the door is shut and I run back to the dining room where I find Prunella lying on the floor with Boo Boo holding the trifle dish on her head and Estelle screaming. Uncle comes running in shortly after with Mr Hookeye.

"What the bloody hell is going on here?"

Prunella stands up, wiping trifle from her face, crying. "That nasty little bitch, Daddy. She attacked me!"

"Yes, Daddy. Prunella is telling the truth," cries Estelle. "I saw everything."

Uncle Grubweed picks Boo Boo up and takes her upstairs and tells her to go to bed. Guardian follows and slumps himself outside the door. I follow and wait a while before going into Boo Boo's room. She is sitting on her bed, playing with her frog puppet.

"Boo Boo, what happened with Prunella?"

"She kicked Guardian," she says, and looks away from me and continues playing quite happily with the puppet.

I go back downstairs and find Mr Hookeye smoking his pipe in the herb garden.

"Quite a bad-tempered little sister you have," he says.

"Don't speak about Boo Boo like that," I say, surprised by the anger in my voice.

"England puts angry little girls away in madhouses." And for the first time he smiles, rather pleased with himself.

That night I hear whispering in Boo Boo's room again. I hear laughing like bells. I dream I am back in the world of water, on the little sailing boat. The water is a mass grave of bodies, shifting in heaped piles of corpses. Bobbling, green and slimy. The sky above me is darkening, clouds become black chimneys. The sun is being eclipsed. The policeman is with me on the boat, standing next to me. Before the sun disappears I see another boat navigating through the dense rolls of rotten flesh. On its mast hangs a moon-shaped lantern, which glows liquid soft blue light and its white sail is covered in red hearts. Mr Loveheart is its captain and he is waving at me.

I wake up to the sound of screaming. I immediately go downstairs to investigate. It is Mrs Treacle who is hysterical. She is standing in the kitchen over the dead body of Mr Icarus Hookeye. His decapitated head is positioned a few feet away from him, next to a wicker basket of potatoes, with a look of astonishment fixed in his eyes.

State of shock?

An urgent telegram is sent to Scotland Yard for the assistance of the police. The reaction of the household is unusually varied. Cornelius, Estelle and Prunella are quite excited by the strange death and are eventually confined to their rooms for their own safety with their mother. Grandpa thinks it is hilarious and is brought downstairs to sit in the living room as he wants to hear everything that is going on.

Uncle Grubweed panics and leaves the house to inform the Professor. Mrs Treacle and Sally refuse to go back into the kitchen, and Boo Boo is quiet as a mouse, playing with Guardian near the woods.

Someone in the house is a murderer. Someone has chopped Mr Hookeye's head off.

I wonder if it rolled along the floor? I wonder if

the murderer had been tempted to kick it like a ball through the window?

I wonder why I am thinking such things.

Constable Walnut and myself are travelling in a very unsteady pony and trap driven by the pub landlord's son. It amazes me that the contraption hasn't collapsed and we haven't all fallen into a ditch. It's kept going by sheer force of will.

The telegram arrived late morning and we dispatched immediately. Detective Waxford was supposed to be assigned the case, as he has previous experience with this village and its inhabitants. But he has a broken foot, due to chasing and capturing an infamous pickpocket of Camden, who made the mistake of "fingering" Waxford, hopeful for a gold pocket watch. Instead he was pursued, thrown into a slop heap outside a butcher's yard and arrested. Waxford, a short Welshman, barrel-shaped with a dark beard, is renowned for his fiery temper, dogged persistence, and great love of poetry. Waxford has previously visited the village Darkwound on four separate occasions, and I am fully aware of the "missing people" cases which have amassed over the years. I have the notes of Waxford's journal on his previous cases and have read over them on the train. I am curious if there might be a connection.

Over the last five years in the village of Darkwound there have been three cases of grave robbings, eight disappearances and three sets of body parts found in the woods. No arrest has been made despite a vigilant investigation by Waxford. There has simply not been enough evidence. His frustration is apparent in his journals, and he has pointed to three individuals whom he finds suspicious. Waxford's prime suspect was initially Lord Loveheart. Surprise, surprise. Waxford had described him as *"a nut"*, *"off his head"* and *"certifiably insane"*.

In his first interview, Mr Loveheart had pretended to be dead. And that, by all accounts, was the most productive of their interviews. So exasperated was Waxford with him that he nearly shot him outside the Vicarage.

It has been many months since I have seen Mr Loveheart, although we had been sent an invitation to his birthday (we were stuck in Wales at the time). I order the landlord's son to drive by Loveheart manor en route to the Grubweed residence.

Waxford's second suspect is Mr Grubweed, the retired undertaker, who now is incredibly wealthy. Waxford had suspected Grubweed of criminal activities as he had been involved in fraud when he was in London – some rumours of illicit grave digging, but nothing solid to arrest him.

Finally Waxford had pointed a heavy finger at Professor Hummingbird. His note – "*I am convinced the Professor is employing Grubweed in some nefarious scheme*" – was scribbled in the margins. But, once again, no evidence strong enough to support any allegations of anything criminal against him; a very frustrated Detective Waxford returned to London and was reassigned.

Before we have even arrived at the Loveheart estate, Mr Loveheart leaps out of the bushes and onto the cart.

"Detective Sergeant White and Constable Walnut. I am so happy to see you both again." In his hands is a bouquet of wild flowers, which he hands to Walnut.

"Thank you very much," says Walnut, looking genuinely pleased.

"So, you've come because of the murder. It's terribly exciting, isn't it ? And no it wasn't me, before you ask. I had nothing to do with it at all."

"What about the missing villagers?"

"I may have decapitated a few undesirables. I believe they were running a demonic cult in the woods. A lot of singing going on; dreadful business."

"A demonic cult, you say?"

"Yes. Simply ghoulish! The chanting went on for hours. And the group harmonies were diabolical."

"There's a cult next door to Scotland Yard," Walnut adds helpfully. "Lots of suspicious droning on a Sunday morning."

"That's not a cult, Walnut, it's a church," I interrupt.

"Well, it sounds unnatural."

"Did you know Icarus Hookeye?" I ask Loveheart.

The driver looks round. "Do you want me to turn about, sir, and head for the Grubweed house?" He stares at Mr Loveheart, the village madman, with a bemused look.

"Yes, thank you," I reply.

"I never met him but I heard terrible things about him. He was the Professor's doctor. Did some work with Grubweed."

"What sort of work?"

"Transportation of bodies, so dark rumours tell me."

"For what?"

"Illegal medical experimentation seems a little predictable to me. My guess would be something more sinister."

"Any proof?"

"Alas, I am not a detective. That is your forte."

"Anything else, Loveheart?"

"Go and visit Mrs Charm. Her chutneys are wonderful," and he throws himself off the carriage, nearly catching his foot, and, lucky as a cat, lands quite gracefully into a bed of primroses as our cart judders onwards. Walnut smells his flowers and smiles.

We arrive at three thirty exactly at the Grubweed residence. We are taken straight to the body by Mrs Treacle and her daughter, Sally, the maid. A white bed sheet has been laid over him with a tea towel over the head.

"I just couldn't bear looking at it, sorry."

I remove the sheet and tea towel.

"Suicide?" Walnut remarks. Mrs Treacle gazes at him, horrified.

I slap Walnut round the back of the head and turn to Mrs Treacle. "Who found the body?"

She averts her eyes from the corpse. "I came

down at six this morning and found him exactly as you see him, sir. He was a dinner guest and business associate of Mr Grubweed. Stayed the night. His room was on the second floor, with the blue door."

The head has been cleanly chopped off. I go through the man's pockets and find a small notebook, a pair of pound notes and a pipe, some tobacco and a key, all of which I remove. There is no sign of a struggle. The head has been taken off in one swipe by an axe or long knife and it was a surprise attack, judging simply by the man's expression. It would have taken someone strong to get a head off in one blow; it was most expertly done. I search the kitchen for the possible murder weapon, but to no avail.

"Walnut, arrange for the removal of the body to the coroner's and start a search of the house and surrounding area for an axe or large bladed weapon."

"Yes, sir."

I take Mrs Treacle and Sally outside into the herb garden and we sit down on a set of chairs around a table.

"Tell me the events of last night?"

"He arrived at eight and had dinner with Mr Grubweed and the children. I believe he retired for the night about midnight."

"How?"

Sally answered, "I passed him on the stairs going into his room. I had just been checking on Grandpa. Their rooms are next to each other."

"Did either of you notice anything peculiar happen during the evening?"

Sally answered, "Not really. Mr Grubweed and Mr Hookeye retired to the study to discuss business after dinner. There was a fight that broke out between the children soon after but apart from that nothing unusual."

"What sort of fight?"

"Miss Boo Boo attacked Miss Prunella, stuck her head in the trifle dish. I didn't witness it, just heard about it after."

"But Mr Hookeye didn't have an argument with anyone that evening?"

"Not that we know of sir," replies Mrs Treacle.

"And your opinion of Mr Hookeye?"

They glance at one another doubtfully. Mrs Treacle responds first. "He wasn't very friendly."

"He was a rude bugger," snaps Sally. Her mother glances worriedly at her. "I only met him a few times, but he was never nice to anyone. Smug and slippery."

"What sort of business were Mr Grubweed and Mr Hookeye involved with?"

"Something to do with the Professor. Mr Hookeye visited us every few months," says Mrs Treacle.

"And the work?"

"I don't know, sir." Sally also shakes her head.

"Do you know of anyone who would want to have harmed Mr Hookeye?"

"No," they say in unison, both shaking their heads.

"Thank you, ladies. And now I would very much like to interview Mr Grubweed."

"He's not here, sir," says Sally, "He's visiting the Professor, but he should be back for his dinner. Mrs Grubweed and Grandpa are in the lounge though. I'll take you there."

Blind Grandpa sits on an old rocking chair in the centre of the room, a knitted blanket on his lap. His daughter, Mrs Grubweed, sits demurely beside him, staring at the wall.

"Good afternoon. I am Detective Sergeant White from Scotland Yard."

"Where's Waxford?" says Grandpa.

"He's broken his foot. If I could ask you some questions?" Mrs Grubweed is still staring at the wall.

"Mrs Grubweed?"

"Oh, ignore her," Grandpa replies, and points at his brain with his finger. "Gone with the fairies."

"Excuse me?"

"You won't get anything out of her. She's always been this way. Never said a word from the day she was born. Never cried as a baby."

I look at her carefully. She still avoids my eyes. "Well, is there anything you would like to tell me Mr…"

"Richard Applecore. That is my name but I am usually referred to as Grandpa. I spend most of my time in my room upstairs or in the garden. I am looked after by my daughter and Sally. I was brought down here after the murder. I tell you, this village is cursed, but it's never boring."

"Did you hear Mr Hookeye leave his room at any point during the night?"

"I heard him go to bed about midnight, because my clock chimed twelve. I slept soundly through the night, so I have no idea when he got up. If you're wondering if I might know who would want him dead, I have no idea. My son-in-law relied on him for work with the Professor, so I would find it strange if he had killed him. Mr Hookeye was a rather dislikeable fellow, but to chop his head off is a rather bold statement."

"What work did he do with your son-in-law?"

"Something to do with corpses for the students at the university; to practise cutting up. People can request their body to be donated for research for medical advancement. My son-in-law has a lot of connections through his previous work as an undertaker."

"Really. I believe Professor Hummingbird is an expert on anthropology, so why is he involved?"

"You'd better ask him," Grandpa Applecore replies.

"Can you tell me anything about the Professor?"

"Very little. And I may be blind, but I am not an idiot, Inspector. My son-in-law is a greedy but stupid man. If you are looking to cast your net for the killer, don't waste your time with the tuna... go and talk to the shark."

"And why do you consider the Professor involved?"

"Call it a gut instinct."

"I would very much like to interview the children, perhaps separately, considering the fight yesterday."

"They are all in their rooms."

Prunella and Estelle share a large room on the second floor, next to their brother and parents. The girls sit playing with their dolls on the floor. A sandy haired rocking horse sits in the corner of the room. Both girls are stout and possibly twins.

"Young ladies, I am from Scotland Yard and I have come to ask you some questions about Mr Hookeye."

"Is he really dead?" asks Prunella, excitedly.

"Yes," I reply.

"How?"

"It appears someone cut off his head."

Both girls' eyes light up. "Uuurrggggghhhhhh!" they say together.

"Did either of you see or hear anything strange last night?"

Prunella shakes her head and Estelle speaks. "We both went to bed at ten o'clock and went straight to sleep."

"Neither of you left your room at any point during the night?"

"No, sir," says Estelle.

"What did you think of Mr Hookeye?"

"Boring," replies Prunella.

"Yes, boring," mimicked Estelle.

"That's incredibly helpful," I say, wearily. And I leave them to it. I'm not going to get anything useful from them.

I knock and enter Cornelius's room. He is sitting

on his bed, carving a piece of wood with a little knife, shaping it into the form of a man.

"Hello, Cornelius. I am–"

"I know who you are," he interrupts me, not looking up from his carving.

"I need to–"

"I don't know who killed Mr Hookeye. I don't know anything. I don't care that he's dead."

"If you know anything that might assist my investigation, you need to tell me."

He remains silent, continuing to carve the little wood man. I step closer to him. He stabs the little doll in the head. "Like I said, detective, I don't know."

I shut the door and leave him to his voodoo.

A young boy approaches me in the hallway. He is small for his age, with a smooth, round face and nut-coloured hair. He shakes my hand. "Pedrock. Age ten. Mr Grubweed is my Uncle."

"Nice to meet you Pedrock. My name is Detective Sergeant White. Is there anything you know that could help with our enquiries?"

"Mr Hookeye and Mr Grubweed were arguing last night about the Professor. I heard Uncle say '*He will drag us both to hell*'. Mr Hookeye threatened to have my sister committed to a madhouse."

"Anything else, Pedrock?"

"Yes, inspector," and Pedrock looks worried, "yes, there is something. I keep hearing noises at night coming from my sister's bedroom. She is only six and I hear something talking to her at night. I went in her room, but I found nothing, I am worried that…"

"I understand. And I will look into it for you."

"Thank you so much, sir."

Constable Walnut comes up the stairs. "The body has been removed for the physician. No sign of the murder weapon so far, sir."

"Thank you, Walnut." I open the door to Boo Boo's room. She is sitting on the floor, playing with a large axe covered in blood.

"Good God," I say under my breath. I approach her softly. "Boo Boo, please give me the axe." And she does, without any problem. I hand it to Constable Walnut who says quietly, "Well that was unexpected."

She is smiling, the little thing. Black eyes, black hair. There is something unusual about her that reminds me of an insect. But, she is six years old. She does not have the strength to wield an axe, let alone cut a head off. She looks up and me and points to Walnut and laughs.

"Funny face!"

"Yes, he does have a funny face, Boo Boo. I am a police detective. My name is Percival. Can you tell me where you got the axe from?"

She shakes her head.

"Did you find the axe?"

She shakes her head.

"Did someone give you the axe?"

She doesn't reply.

"Boo Boo, who is talking to you at night?"

"An angel," she says, her eyes bright and dark like liquid chocolate.

I crouch next to her. "What does the angel look like?"

She touches my nose with her finger. "Like you," she says.

"He's a man. What is his name?"

"Mr Angelcakes," and she smiles a big soppy smile and cuddles me.

I meet with Constable Walnut in the herb garden.

"Everything alright, sir?" he enquires.

"Yes. I want you to ask Sally to make arrangements for us to stay at the Highwayman public house in the village tonight. And get her to send this telegram." I hand him the note.

DETECTIVE WAXFORD
CAN WE MEET? VERY STRANGE
SITUATION HERE.
DETECTIVE SERGEANT WHITE

"Are you arresting the six year-old?"

"No. Someone is manipulating her and making a fool of us."

I go back into the house and inspect the guest room of Icarus Hookeye. The room is comfortable, if small. The bed unmade with gentlemen's toiletries by the mirror and washbasin. His coat hangs behind the door. I go through the pockets, only finding some matches. Nothing else. It is then that I examine the pocket book I found on his body. A little red book, and what a curious thing it is! On every page is a sketch of a black butterfly. Over and over. Butterfly after black butterfly. They soar across the pages in inky shapes. Snap shut their wings at the edges, glide over white spaces. Is this some sort of code? Does this have secret meaning?

Detective Sergeant White & Constable Walnut interview the Professor

We trudge through the undergrowth towards the medieval keep of the Professor and arrive just as the sun is beginning to set. I have borrowed a lantern from Mrs Treacle for our return journey. The woods round this area are especially sinister. An owl hoots in the distance.

"Any theories, Walnut, on our killer?"

"Nothing is springing to mind, sir."

The moated keep materialises in front of us. White-moon-coloured flowers float on the waters. We cross the bridge and walk into the courtyard, approach a little side door. To my surprise, it is open and we enter. The corridor is blood red: the wallpaper red, the carpet red, the ceiling red. It is like stepping through a tunnel of blood. Inside an intestine. Red upon red. Red, they say, is the colour of magic. The colour of devils.

This is a labyrinth maze. A coiling puzzle of corridors, each leading to a room of red. And along the walls are framed glass pictures, each with a butterfly with a pin through its heart.

To stop you flying away, you naughty thing

There are hundreds of them, each different. Chocolate browns, fuzzy pinks, lemon curd yellows, peacock blues. We keep moving: red upon red surrounds us, enclosing upon us. More butterflies trapped in glass.

"This is some sort of madness," I say to Constable Walnut.

Finally, the corridor coils, spiral shaped, into a room at the centre, the heart of this diabolical maze. Here sits Professor Hummingbird at his study desk, writing in his journal. Behind him is an enormous butterfly, the wing span of two human hands. It is ebony black with two red shaped eyes on the wings.

"You are admiring my prize possession," the Professor remarks, and he raises his head. His voice is soothing and oddly mesmeric. He is a man in his late fifties, I would have guessed; he sports a long beard and has deep amber eyes. He wears striped trousers and pointy blue slippers.

"She is the rarest butterfly in the world and I have

the only specimen. She's a dazzler, isn't she? Originates from Mexico. Her name translates as 'Angel-Eater'. She eats other butterflies."

"I am Detective Sergeant White and this is Constable Walnut. I believe Mr Grubweed may be here?"

"You just missed him. He left rather upset. He was very close to Icarus."

"You're aware of the situation then?"

"Of course. My associate has been decapitated." The Professor smiles.

"Do you know of anyone that would want to harm him?"

"Not at all. He was quite an amusing fellow and competent doctor."

"And can you account for your whereabouts last night?"

"I was here the entire evening, writing my journals. I have no alibi. I have only one servant, my housekeeper, who comes in the mornings. I prefer as little human interaction as possible. I can only work with my butterflies with absolutely no other distraction."

"What sort of work was he doing for you?" I step closer.

"Menial tasks. Paper pushing, administrative

silliness." He yawned.

"Procurement of body parts for medical research?" I add.

"Oh, he wasn't that macabre. You see devils, sergeant, when there are only men."

"Perhaps, but something bizarre is happening," I state.

Walnut points to the Angel-Eater. "Blimey! She's still alive!" The Angel-Eater is beating its wings against the glass.

The Professor strokes the glass. "She's excitable today. It would be for the best if you both left us in peace now." And he points a finger at the door.

I take my pistol out and point it at his head. "You're coming in for questioning."

The Professor pounds his fists on his desk. The walls move, ripple like water.

Zap!

We are transported in a flash of blue light to The Highwayman pub.

The locals are staring at us, their eyeballs on stalks. I put my pistol down. "Walnut, what just happened?"

"I don't know, sir, but I could murder a pint."

After a few moments recovering from the shock, we eat meat pies and mash and wash it down with plenty of ale.

"So we're dealing with a sorcerer?" Walnut sighs.

"It looks that way. I should have known we'd get something peculiar. He is one of Loveheart's neighbours."

"Well, we've met some odd balls before, sir."

That night, I dream I am in the Grubweed kitchen with Boo Boo, and she has a knife in her little hands. On the table is a cake, yellow and pink sponge, and she is slicing it, and blood is oozing out and dripping on the floor.

"Angel food cake," she giggles, and I open my eyes.

When I wake up two things occur. A telegram arrives back from Detective Waxford:

PERCIVAL
    COME BACK INTO LONDON AND MEET,
  38 BIZWIT STREET, NR BAKER STREET.
    HENRY WAXFORD

Walnut taps me on the shoulder. "Mr Grubweed has not returned home. He's officially missing."

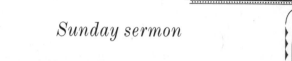

Sunday sermon

I hold my sister's hand as Mrs Treacle escorts us to church, Guardian the dog following. The church is about half full. I recognize Mrs Charm and the landlord's son and his parents. Mrs Treacle points out Mr Pinhole, the apothecary, a weedy looking man near the back row, and Mr and Mrs Tufflehump who own the bakery. The air is cool inside the church and little blue flowers have been placed round the pews. Mr Wormhole ascends the pulpit, flaming eyed, and a respectful silence ensues.

He shakes his head wearily. "Murder!" he cries, arms raised. "Bloody murder! The devil is here in our village. He walks amongst us! Perhaps he hops amongst us; he may even LIMP!"

A voice behind me mumbles, "He's been on the rum again."

Revered Wormhole holds a stiff finger aloft. "FEAR NOT, THE LORD WILL STOMP A MIGHTY FOOT ON THE VILLAIN. SQUASH HIM INTO THE GROUND, MAKE HIM A SPLAT!"

The congregation gasp, and I can hear Mrs Charm comment to Mrs Tufflehump, "He's definitely improved."

Mr Wormhole continues, "Pray to the Lord to reveal this monster. Show his face to us oh Lord! Help the policemen from London arrest, charge and execute! Oh merciful God, make sure this evil creature is flogged repeatedly in the hell fires. Save us from further decapitation!"

Much nodding of agreement from the heads of the congregation. I turn my head and I can see Mr Loveheart, dressed in lemon curd yellow, standing by the door. He waggles a finger for me to come over to him. Red hearts are all over his waistcoat. I slip away unnoticed while Wormhole begins protestations about being roasted to death by devils with forked tongues and large cooking implements.

Mr Loveheart and I walk out into the graveyard and the dazzling sunshine.

"I thought I had better warn you," says Loveheart.

"Of what?"

"I think your uncle is dead and I believe the

Professor has some sinister plan for your sister."

"What can I do?" I say.

"You're too little, Pedrock. Fear not! I have managed to acquire a bomb and I am thinking of blowing him up," laughs Mr Loveheart.

I really don't know how to respond to that remark.

Detective White & Detective Waxford compare notes

I find Bizwit Street after some initial confusion. I had travelled down to London immediately after receiving Waxford's telegram and have left Constable Walnut to take statements from the villagers to see if he can acquire any further information. I knock on number 38 and Henry Waxford, hobbling, opens the door.

"Come in, Percival." His voice is like roasting wood on a fire, spitting and cracking.

We sit in a very comfy study surrounded by his book collection, and he hands me a glass of whisky, props his foot up on a cushion and stares at me.

"So, how is the case developing?"

"Professor's physician found decapitated in Mr Grubweed's house and now Mr Grubweed is missing; they both worked for the Professor. The murder weapon, an axe, was found in the hands of a six year-old cousin, Boo Boo, who claims a man called Mr Angelcakes is visiting her at night."

"This is a wicked business," growls Waxford. He sinks back his whisky. "And that Professor has everything to do with it. Have you interviewed him yet? Seen his butterflies?"

"Yes, yes, it was bizarre. His house is a maze and it appears the Professor dabbles in the occult: he managed to evict myself and Walnut from his property using..." – I pause – "some sort of black magic."

Waxford looks a little shocked. "Black magic? More like trickery, Percival. They're all nuts in that village. Especially that bloody Mr Loveheart."

"Loveheart can be extremely cooperative. You just have to humour him."

"I'm glad I don't have to go back there." Waxford sighs. "It would have driven me mad."

"I have been reading your journals and they have been most helpful. Is there anything you left out which could aid me now?"

Waxford wiggles his bandaged foot. "I tried to research the Professor and it was very difficult. He has two family members alive. A wife, Lucy, who is in a madhouse. Her full name is Lucy Dewdoll. By all accounts she didn't go mad until she married him. And guess who one of the doctors was who signed the certificate to condemn her?"

"Hookeye?"

"Yes. And she's the sixth wife he's had."

"Good God, what happened to the rest?"

"I couldn't find out. I was sure I was being followed at the time. Not a scrap of proof. His brother is Ignatius Hummingbird, who holds a seat in the House of Lords and has influence with the prime minister. I'm afraid Professor Hummingbird is very well protected."

"Where is his wife now?"

"Well, they are divorced due to her madness and she resides in the Blue-Flower Institution near Blackheath. But she may have information for you which might help. She is the only lead I can think of."

"Thank you, Waxford. Tell me, what do you think he's up to, the Professor? What's really going on?"

"There were a lot of suspicions at the time. The main line of thinking was that Hookeye and Grubweed were providing bodies for experimentation. The question was how they were getting these bodies. But I can't see the reason for the Professor to have any interest in such a thing. He's obsessed with his butterflies and his research on the Aztecs. No, in my opinion there is something else going on."

"I found a little red diary in Icarus Hookeye's coat pocket. Inside were numerous drawings of butterflies."

"What meaning could that have, other than a connection to the Professor?" Waxford asked.

"That's what I wondered." I help myself to a refill of whisky and top Waxford up.

"Why kill Icarus and Grubweed?"

"Maybe someone is picking them off," I say instinctively, and suddenly I feel quite odd.

"Percival, are you alright?" Waxford leans forward.

"Yes. I just had the strangest feeling."

The Blue-Flower Institute

I am, I admit, a little drunk after seeing Waxford. He has a more robust constitution for alcohol. I buy some strong coffee and make my way to the reception area of the Blue-Flower Institute, a miserable-looking building. A largely built woman with fierce little eyes examines me at the front desk.

"My name is Detective Sergeant White. I need to see a resident. A woman named Lucy Dewdoll. It is quite urgent and involves a murder investigation."

I am escorted to a cell where Lucy Dewdoll sits at a small table in a long grey dress. Her hair, loose and falling to her waist, is the colour of dirty sand. Her face is like her name: doll-like, perfect skin and round blue eyes. She turns to look at me.

"Please get me out of here."

"Miss Dewdoll, I understand that you were

married to Professor Hummingbird. I am currently investigating a murder and I need to know whatever you can tell me, anything that might give me some insight into his character."

"If I do this, can you get me out of here? I am not mad. I have never been mad."

"I will do everything in my power to help you."

"If you want any power over him, detective, steal his favourite butterfly. It is his only weakness."

"My dear lady, what happened to you?" I ask, and then I listen.

"I was living with my stepsister in Whitstable when I met him. The year was 1886. I was twenty-five and our life was peaceful, unremarkable, until a letter arrived from a solicitor in London called Mr Evening-Star, announcing that I had been left a fortune from my eccentric Uncle Lionel, who was an explorer in Mexico. I had become his heiress, owner of a moated castle on the outskirts of London, as well as inheriting his entire collection of artefacts from his explorations. Well, I nearly fainted on the carpet I was so shocked! Winnie thankfully retrieved the emergency brandy from under the cupboard." A slight smile danced across her face at the memory, and then vanished just as quickly. "The following day I received a visitor, a friend of my

Uncle Lionel, who wished to offer his condolences. His name was Professor Gabriel Hummingbird. He was a widower in his fifties and there was something unusual about him, some strange, cool mischief. The way he looked at me – as though he were peering down a microscope, examining my cells, wanting to rearrange them. We talked at length about my uncle's work in Mexico and then finally about his own research. They had worked together for years teaching at the University in London. My uncle had died while camping on an Inca burial site, slipped and fell off a ravine while drunk on chocolate-wine. His body had been buried out there, the service simple, but in accordance with my uncle's wishes, according to Professor Hummingbird.

"The Professor informed me that he would be staying in Whitstable for a few weeks as a holiday and hoped we should meet again. Apart from the fact that he was too old for me, there was something else about him that made me concerned. There was something mechanical, something calculating about him. I was persuaded he did not desire me; however, I was an heiress now. Perhaps it was my money, perhaps something else I had acquired, and yet despite all these warning signals I agreed to see him again, and again. It was almost as if I could not say the word 'No' to him. The word just would not form on my lips.

"We met for tea and sandwiches and walked along the beach, picking up curious shells. I told him about my quiet but happy life, but thinking about my Uncle Lionel, I realised how little I had actually lived. How empty my background appeared in comparison with the Professor, who regaled me with tales of his hunting for rare butterflies in Peru and getting lost knee deep in a swamp while being chased by local tribesmen.

"On our third meeting he proposed and I accepted. I knew I had made a mistake when I said the word 'yes'. I knew and yet I said it anyway and did not retract."

She sobbed and I put my hand in hers, and after some time she regained her composure and wiped her eyes, "We were married in a small church by the sea. Our honeymoon was spent at our moated castle and the..." – she paused – "...the wedding night was..."

She stopped and looked at me, "It is only the butterflies that excite him."

She continued, "He had every wall in the castle painted red as though we were walking in tunnels of blood and on every wall nothing but his butterflies. Row after row of them. And his favourite he hung in his study.

"One evening we received two guests for dinner: both medical doctors. Icarus Hookeye and Sebastian Crabmouth. I should have known what he was planning. The wine was drugged. I was transported to the Blue-Flower Institution for the insane and have been here for over two years."

"I am going to get you out of here," I said.

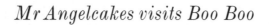

Mr Angelcakes visits Boo Boo

He has come again to see me. The lovely, mad Mr Angelcakes. He only comes at night. He comes when people are sleeping.

Tonight he starts to carve something into my back. It hurts a lot. He says:

Ssssshhhhhhh
Boo Boo. Don't be afraid. I am
the angel man. It's only a
butter
fly...

Lady Beetle's garden party

Nobody knows where Uncle Grubweed is, but I think Mr Loveheart is right. He's probably dead and his corpse will turn up at some point. Grandpa says we still have to go to the party. That's what Uncle would have wanted and we will finally get to meet handsome Horatio. Horatio the prize, Horatio the favourite. I already know I won't like him. I already know. When I imagine him I think of the red-black juices of overripe tomatoes; squelchy, fat and bloated. There's something squashed and damaged about him.

We are all dressed up in our best clothes. I had to borrow something from Cornelius and it's too big, so Mrs Treacle had to sew it. Boo Boo has a little black dress which Prunella used to wear, and Mrs Treacle has added a red ribbon to her hair. Boo Boo and I are to arrive a little later than everyone else as we will be attending with Reverend Plum, who is late as he missed his train.

We sit on the steps of the house with Guardian, whose soft paws rest on my lap, nuzzling me with his nose. Boo Boo keeps scratching her back, says it itches. The policemen are going to the party too. They still haven't found out who killed Mr Hookeye.

"Boo Boo," I look at her, "who is Mr Angelcakes?"

She stops scratching and looks at her feet. "I am not allowed to say," she replies.

"Why not?" But she doesn't answer and I hear the pony and trap clattering along the path, carrying Reverend Plum, who is waving at us. We gingerly step aboard and Guardian lies by Boo Boo's feet, his eyeballs staring lovingly up at her as though she's a delicious chicken leg.

Reverend Plum asks, "How have you been, children? Has anything exciting happened?"

I was tempted for a moment not to answer him.

"Doctor Hookeye got his head cut off in the kitchen and the police from Scotland Yard are here, and they found Boo Boo with the murder weapon and Uncle Grubweed has gone missing, presumed also murdered. We are both well, thank you. How was your trip?"

The Reverend Plum goes into a funny trance for the rest of the journey.

The garden party sits beneath an achingly hot sun. It looks to me like a fried egg sizzling in a pan. A great long table with blackberry-coloured sheets holds plates of wonderful roast pork sandwiches, plum and cream cakes, jellies, overripe peaches and fat strawberries, meat pies and pickles. There is champagne, cider, pink wine and apple juice to drink.

The feast is hovered over by heavy bees, occasionally flicked away by an exasperated manservant. Lady Beetle is wearing a long, pale blue dress and she stands with her son, also in pale blue, in the centre of the gardens. They are chatting to a gentleman I haven't seen before, a man with stripy trousers. I can see Prunella and Estelle eating jelly, sitting under a tree with their mother, carefully watching Horatio as a blackbird would watch a worm. Looking forward to eating him. Two princesses squabbling over a prince.

Mrs Charm, wearing a huge sun hat with lavender sprigs, is sitting at a table talking with Mr Loveheart, who today is wearing bright orange. So bright is the orange that he is nearly outshining the sun. It almost hurts my eyes to look at him. Red hearts are dotted about his waistcoat and a large slice of cake sits in his hands. Mr Wormhole, lurking in the shadows, is eating a cream cake very happily and chatting to Detective White and Constable Walnut.

Boo Boo and I approach Mrs Beetle as Reverend Plum has wandered off in the direction of the policemen.

"Thank you for inviting us to your party, Lady Beetle," I say.

She looks at me, rather bored. The older man next to her smiles. He has very odd eyes. They are ancient and full of ghosts. It is like looking into a dead thing.

"Hello," he says,. "My name is Professor Hummingbird," and he shakes my hand.

"I am sorry that your friend was decapitated in our kitchen," I reply, and Mrs Beetle looks mortified.

The Professor smiles, "It's not your fault. I am sure they will catch the culprit." He turns his attention towards Boo Boo, who is trying to scratch her back and is red eyed. "Are you alright, little girl?"

"My back hurts," she says.

"Let me take a look at it." She turns round and he unbuttons the back of her dress. "It might be a bee sting," he says, and then opens the back. His hands start to shake. On her back is an inky huge black butterfly with red eyes.

"How did you get this on your back?" He can barely withhold his excitement.

"Mr Angelcakes did it."

The Professor, containing his emotions, re-buttons her dress and walks off towards Reverend Plum. Boo Boo runs off to play with Guardian. What is happening to her? What can I do to stop it?

Horatio Beetle then steps forward and shakes my hand. The prince in pale blue has black hair and eyes like dark water. "You must be Pedrock. I've been away in Cambridge most of the summer. There's nothing to do much round here anyway. Boring little place." He yawns. "I think your uncle had some fantasy to marry me off eventually to one of his fat daughters." And he laughs and I notice a beauty spot below his nose. It occurs to me that *he's marked*. I suppose he is really very handsome, much like a prince in a fairy story, but I wouldn't want my sister to marry him. "My mother tells me you and your sister are poor little orphans. You look like pig-farming peasants! Oink oink! Keep your piggy fingers out of my cakes," and he laughs. What a shitbag he is.

A scotch egg soars through the air. Smacks him in the face. "Ouch!" he screams, followed by a wail of *"Mother!"*

I look for the person responsible and see naughty Mr Loveheart waving at me, the sunlight bouncing off him, vying for attention. How bright he is. What sort of magic is he?

I step away from Horatio, move out of his orbit.

I help myself to the buffet, piling my plate with an assortment until it wobbles about. Consider throwing it over Horatio's head. And then I move towards Mrs Charm and Mr Loveheart who are engaged in a deep conversation about apricot jam.

"Hello," I say.

"Pedrock, darling!" Mrs Charm cries. "Come and sit with us." And so I plop myself down.

"What do you think of Horatio?"

"Vain and spoilt," I reply quietly.

"Quite right too. I am going to write him into my novel. Perhaps have him disembowelled. Don't you think Mr Loveheart looks very fetching today?"

"Will you write him into your novel as well?"

"Of course, he's something wicked and something wonderful."

"Hello again," Loveheart waggles what appears to be a gherkin at me and then pops it into his mouth.

"Mr Loveheart," the Professor says, standing behind him. "Mr Loveheart, I don't think we've been introduced. But I have heard *so* much about you."

"Likewise," replies Loveheart. They stare at one another, Mr Loveheart remaining seated.

The Professor then glances over to me. "Pedrock, I have spoken to Reverend Plum regarding the sad recent events and we both agree that it would be in Boo Boo's best interests if she came to live with me."

I am horrified.

"Would it really?" replies Mr Loveheart, darkly.

"Is it wise to separate a brother and sister?" cries Mrs Charm. "Surely that is not for the best."

"Pedrock can see Boo Boo whenever he wishes and Reverend Plum is their legal guardian until Mr Grubweed reappears. The decision is made, I'm afraid."

I am crying and I can't help it. Mrs Charm puts her arm around me.

"There is no need to be upset, Pedrock." The Professor's voice is smooth like velvet.

"There is every reason," and Loveheart stands up to face him.

"Do we have a problem, Mr Loveheart?"

"Not if you're dead."

The Professor momentarily loses his composure and then, quickly regaining it, he says, "I really am quite disappointed in you, I thought you of all people would understand." And he turns to leave, walking into the shade, the darkness obscuring his features.

"Don't you worry," says Mrs Charm, gently. "Mr Loveheart will sort this mess out."

Mr Loveheart yawns lazily, his feet resting on the table, and waggles his sword in the direction of the Professor, "Disembowelled perhaps? Mmmmm…"

I spend the remainder of the party crying into Mrs Charm's lap. Boo Boo wanders over and puts her hand on my cheek. "Pedrock, please can you take care of Guardian? The Professor won't let me take him."

I nod my head sadly and she cuddles me and then leaves, hand in hand with the Professor, a little girl and a monster.

Mrs Charm is muttering, "He's a villain."

That night in bed I wait to hear whispering in Boo Boo's room, but nothing comes. Guardian now sleeps in my room and howls most of the night in sadness. I close my eyes and make a wish that Mr Loveheart will kill the Professor. I wish and wish and wish and when I open my eyes there is a boy sitting on the end of my bed with eyes of black glitter.

"Who are you?" I say, rubbing the sleep from my eyes.

"Death." His voice is as soft as moth wings.

"What do you want with me?"

"Your sister will be able to take care of herself. You will see her again. Be patient. Be very patient."

"He's going to hurt her, I know it," I cry.

"And someone is going to hurt him." And the boy smiles and it is the most terrifying smile I have ever seen. "Now go back to sleep, Pedrock, and in the morning you will feel better. Go sailing on the lake. Start to live your life. Stop worrying about your sister. Let the Fates deal with the Professor."

"What will happen to him?"

The boy pulls a loose thread from his sleeve and examines it, dropping it casually onto the floor. "A taste of his own particular medicine."

Lucy Dewdoll escapes

I am sitting in my cell, staring at a spider on the wall, its web half done, like a piece of lace, incomplete. There's a tapping at the barred window. I peer out. A man on a ladder with a hacksaw.

"Good morning, Miss Dewdoll. My name is Mr Loveheart – and I'm here to rescue you."

Attempt to steal the butterfly, rescue Boo Boo and blow up the Professor

It's two o'clock in the morning, and Constable Walnut and myself are about to break into the Professor's house. We're hiding in a bush near the moat.

"I've brought my lucky ferret leg, sir," said Walnut, and he whipped out a disgusting, deformed thing from his pocket and held it under my nose

"My God, what happened to that unfortunate creature!?"

There is a rummaging from the bushes and Mr Loveheart appears with a pistol and what appears to be a bomb.

"Lovely evening," he says.

"What the hell are you doing here?" I'm confounded.

"I'm here to rescue Boo Boo and blow the villain up. And you?"

"We're here to steal his favourite butterfly. Can we at least accomplish that before you blow the building up?"

"I'm getting confused," says Walnut, still gripping the ferret leg, "If he's blowing the Professor up, then we don't need to steal the butterfly, do we?"

"Why don't we all go in together. Make it a group effort," says Loveheart, glancing with suspicion at the object in Walnut's hand,

Walnut breaks the side window using a rock and we climb through into one of the hallways and sneak along the passageway, the butterflies above our heads, row upon row like ancestral portraits. The moon is our only light. Walnut occasionally bumps into me.

"What a slum he lives in," Loveheart remarks. "He has no understanding of décor."

"We need to get Boo Boo first," I say, and we ascend a small spiral staircase leading to the upper floor where there are six doors and yet more butterflies. The first room is an empty bedroom used to store the killing jars and poison for the butterflies. Walnut opens the second room, which creaks softly like a haunted house. The room is empty except for the walls where seven photographs in frames sit, each one with a picture of a woman. Each woman wearing a wedding dress. White lace, white smiles, white ghosts. I recognize Lucy Dewdoll immediately: smile shy, awkward, ill-fitting dress, a lizard cream frill round her neck, ruffled, suffocating.

It is the picture that is next to her that worries me more. It is Boo Boo. She is sitting on a chair in the photograph, her little legs dangling. Her shoe wonky, her eyes glazed over as though lost deep in space.

Loveheart glances over my shoulder. "Bride number seven?"

I feel sick to my stomach. We leave that room and proceed to the third. Walnut trips over the carpet, Loveheart commenting, "I feel secure in the knowledge that I am working with professionals."

The third room is an empty nursery with butterfly wallpaper. The fourth room is filled with shelves with hundreds of jars. Loveheart picks one up and examines it curiously.

"What's inside them?" I whisper.

"Dead butterflies," he replies.

"I have this bad feeling, sir," says Constable Walnut.

"Keep it to yourself, Walnut."

It is Loveheart who opens the fifth door, which reveals a massive bedroom where the Professor lies asleep on a huge black four poster bed. His favourite butterfly hangs above his head, as black as space. Soft-footedly Loveheart creeps round the bed and takes the butterfly off the wall while the Professor snores.

I go straight into the last room and find Boo Boo. I pick her up in my arms and carry her down the corridor. Walnut is holding the butterfly and Mr Loveheart is busy placing the bomb under the Professor's bed.

Loveheart comes running out. "Quickly!" he cries, and we all run down the stairs and towards the window. I manage to push Boo Boo out through the window and then turn to see Professor Hummingbird and he's opening his mouth and butterflies are flying out, zooming towards us.

The six wives of Professor Hummingbird

1. *Elizabeth: poisoned with arsenic*
2. *Rowena: pushed down the stairs*
3. *Guinevere: buried alive*
4. *Pandora: committed to an asylum*
5. *Lottie: strangled*
6. *Lucy: committed to an asylum and then escaped*

Detective Waxford returns to Darkwound

I hate this bloody village. My foot has not healed properly and I'm limping about. The morphine takes the pain away at least. I'm on a pony and trap heading for the Professor's home. Detective White, Constable Walnut and Mr Loveheart have been missing for the last week. I am prepared for any eventuality as this part of England is full of mad people. The forests are sinister, dense, stuffed with strange plant life. I was really hoping never to come back to this backwater village with its abnormally high criminal activity.

I had been considering an early retirement from the force: a nice little cottage and an overweight cat for company.

Where are you, Detective White?

We cross the bridge and enter the courtyard to the

Hummingbird moated castle, and there's a little girl drawing with a piece of chalk on the stone slabs.

"Miss," I say.

She ignores me and so I step closer. I see she's drawing butterflies, hundreds of them.

"Miss," I repeat.

She looks up.

"Who are you?" I say.

"My name is Boo Boo. The Professor adopted me."

"Oh, has he now. I am Detective Waxford and I am looking for Detective White, Constable Walnut and Mr Loveheart, who are all currently missing. Have you seen them?"

"Yes. They tried to rescue me and blow the Professor up."

"*Bloody hell.* Where are they?"

She doesn't reply.

"Where is the Professor, Boo Boo?"

She points towards the door.

I draw my gun out and enter the house; that creepy corridor of red and bloody butterflies. I move along the red carpets. All those insects, all those silver pins.

"Where are you, Professor?" I shout.

I move further inside the maze. And I hear, what

is that noise? A tapping, a fluttering, then I finally see. Oh God. The butterflies, all the butterflies are moving. They are alive!

And he suddenly appears from his study smiling, "How can I help you, Detective Waxford?"

"Where are they?" I point the gun at his head.

"Who?" he says softly.

"YOU KNOW WHO. WHERE ARE THEY, YOU FUCKING LUNATIC?!"

"Calm down, detective."

"Professor Hummingbird. I am taking you in for questioning."

"Oh, you're so dramatic," he sighs.

"THIS IS FROM THE MAN WHOSE HOME LOOKS LIKE THE LAIR OF A VILE MURDERER."

"Tut tut, don't get yourself into a tizz-woz."

"I am very happy to blow your demented brain out of your skull right here and dump you in the moat, but I need to know what you've done with them."

He shrugs his shoulders.

"Are they dead?"

He doesn't answer.

"ARE THEY DEAD?" I scream in his ear.

He sticks his tongue out. A tiny green butterfly zooms out of his mouth into the endless red.

Infuriated, I march him at gun point to the pony and trap, where Boo Boo is sat drawing a giant butterfly.

"Boo Boo, come with me," I say, and lift her onto the carriage. The Professor waves goodbye to his butterflies, "Toodle oooooooo."

Professor Hummingbird is questioned at Scotland Yard

The Professor's lawyer, Cedric Evening-Star, arrives to attend the questioning

"I'm so sorry, Cedric," Hummingbird's voice is playful, "I really don't understand how this has happened. I'm not sure what Detective Waxford thinks I've done but this is ridiculous."

"Shut up, Hummingbird. Your adopted daughter told us that Detective White, Constable Walnut and Mr Loveheart were in your house last Sunday early morning to rescue her. That was the last time any of them were seen."

"You mean *kidnap*," he retorts.

"Explain to me what happened."

"I was awoken sometime after two in the morning by footsteps and voices. I noticed when I got up that my prize butterfly had been removed from the wall. I went downstairs and caught sight of Detective White with Boo Boo in his arms, pushing her through a window; Constable Walnut with my butterfly in his hands and Mr Loveheart telling everyone to get out quickly because he'd placed a bomb under my bed."

Cedric Evening-Star added, "So, kidnapping, theft and attempted murder."

"And what happened next?"

"The bomb went off and blew up my bedroom and the entire roof of the keep."

"And?"

"Well, there was a lot of dust in the air and debris falling about and I was confused and dizzy."

"Where is Detective White?"

"I don't know where any of them are. They must have escaped."

"Why is Boo Boo still with you if they escaped?"

"She came back to me. She obviously didn't feel safe with them."

"Do you have the butterfly?"

He pauses for a moment. "Yes, Constable Walnut must have dropped it. I was lucky. It is priceless."

"What total shite," I say.

"I beg your pardon," Cedric Evening-Star gasps.

"It's rather convenient that Boo Boo and your

butterfly are returned to you and three men missing. What did you do to them?"

"Search my house if you must, you won't find them."

"Not without a warrant," adds Mr Evening-Star. "This harassment of my client will stop now."

I leave the room to speak to Boo Boo. She is sitting in my office, waiting for me, drawing butterflies on my desk.

"Boo Boo, tell me the truth. What happened that night?"

She put her piece of chalk down and looks up at me. "Detective White carried me out of bed and put me through a window and told me to run. Then the bomb went off. I waited for them to come out. But none of them did. I ran to the village to see Mrs Charm and she made me hot chocolate. Later the Professor came to take me back to his castle."

"Do you think they are dead?"

"No. He turned them into butterflies."

Zedock Heap has tea with Queen Victoria

I am escorted by a rather frail-looking servant gripping a pink frilled parasol into the gardens of the Queen. Her gardens are full of red roses. Fat heaps of fleshy petals. OPEN FOR ME. OPEN FOR ME. Show me your insides

She is surrounded by her roses. Red within red. You want to understand about power? You want to know what it is? Look at her.

SHE IS COLOSSAL!

Red horns five foot high sprout from her head, curl into points. She wears a dress of dazzling red, and stares at me with the intensity of a flesh eating insect, while an Indian servant fans her with black ostrich feathers. A selection of strawberry tarts and a green pot of tea wait for me.

"Ah, Zedock," she smiles and curls a finger, drawing me closer. She is from Underneath. She is the very core of it. She is the only thing I have ever feared.

I take off my hat and seat myself next to the Queen of England, the Queen of Hell.

I kiss her hand. She pulls me close to her lips. The strength of her, the muscle nearly breaks my bones into dust.

"I am your humble servant, Your Majesty"

"YES YOU ARE, my darling."

I can see inside her mouth. The rows and rows of teeth. How I worship her, how I love her. You are the Master of my heart. Magnificent, magnificent. EATER OF WORLDS.

SUPER CANNIBAL SUPER CANNIBAL All hail QUEEN VICTORIA!

She kisses my lips. I feel planets collide, explode into pieces. Lava hot. When she releases me, she knows all my secrets, she has tasted all my thoughts, my dreams, my wishes.

She pours the tea, and smiles. Oh thou wondrous crocodile! MAN EATER. Feel the chomp, the crunch of bones. Liquidize in her stomach: melt into her middle

"You are the only woman I have any respect for," I say dizzy from her kiss, and I sip my tea, which has a curious aftertaste of meteorite.

"All humans are sausages," she sighs and glances furtively at the servant whose legs are trembling and plops a strawberry tart on a plate and passes it to me.

I thank her, bite into it. Slice it in half with teeth.

"Why are you so worried about little Mr Loveheart, dearest? He's a mad thing, no match for you, my darling."

"He *irks* me," I reply

"You are MY prime minister. You are my commander. You are my champion. FLATTEN HIM, EAT HIM UP," and she stares into me, drags me under. Her red eyes are corridors into Hell: the carpets spongy with blood.

"Of course, my Queen."

"Good boy. Mr Loveheart is edible. What do mad things taste of I wonder? Perhaps he is sweet," and she takes another tart and pops it between her teeth. "You've always been so competitive Zedock," and I know, if she wished it, she could splat me like a bug.

She continues, "But remember: I am the top of the food chain," and she raises her finger to her servant, "Come to me." Her voice is the darkest, most powerful hypnotism. I can feel the pressure; oh wondrous Queen. She is the horror fairytale. The garden shudders under her, ley lines form, fruit explodes in the trees.

The servant puts down the fan rather shakily and walks towards his Queen.

Hell is hungry.

Her gardens are full of red roses. Her gardens are full of blood. See them bloom, see them burst open! Oooooze. Seep their juices onto the lawn:

drip

    drip

       drip.

Lick a petal and you will taste yourself.

PART TWO

Boo Boo grows up
BOO BOO AND MR ANGELCAKES

The first time he visited me, I was six and it was my first night in Uncle Grubweed's house. Pedrock had kissed me goodnight and I was alone. Alone in the sticky blackness, waggling my feet over the end of the bed, examining the space between my toes. I had always wanted red shoes. I remember Sister Harriet at the convent, who smelt of floor polish, told me that witches wear red shoes. I think Sister Harriet is probably dead now.

Mr Angelcakes was wearing another man's skin when he appeared. I thought he was an angel, his eyes were so bright, like firecrackers.

I didn't like the way he was looking at me.

He made bite marks on my arms, said I tasted like ice-cream.

"Do angels eat ice-cream?" I said.

"All **the time**," he replied. "Now don't be afraid, Boo Boo. My name is Mr Angelcakes and I am here to teach you."

"Teach me what?"

"**To** k**ill**."

I cuddled my frog puppet. I squeezed him close to my heart.

"**I am going to make you very strong,** Boo **Boo. I am** going to **m**ake **you into a weapon.**"

"I don't understand," I whispered.

"**T**onight **I am going** to **tell** you **a story**," and he touched my head with his finger, the skin loose and yellowish. I lay on the bed and closed my eyes and listened to the spider-words oozing from his mouth. Hairy, black little words. Tickling me with their fangs.

Once Upon a Time, there was a young man called Mr Angelcakes and he had one thing he loved most in the world: his pet butterfly which was black and red.

But a very bad man called Hummingbird stole his butterfly and locked Mr Angelcakes in a tomb. Mr Angelcakes starved to death. *And then something rather nasty took the* skin off *him and wore it. This nasty thing liked to eat human skins because they made him big and strong. The nasty thing liked the name Mr Angelcakes and decided to keep it.*

So, the new Mr Angelcakes, deciding he wanted the butterfly Hummingbird had stolen, followed him back to England and watched him. The butterfly was very special, it protected Hummingbird from any harm and Mr Angelcakes couldn't get close enough to steal it. The butterfly was believed to be the soul of an Aztec warrior, the greatest warrior of the Empire. She had never been defeated in battle. **For all butterflies are warrior souls.**

And so, Mr Angelcakes waited and watched Hummingbird for many years. Hummingbird liked to collect butterflies and to increase his collection he married women to inherit their butterfly collections and then killed them or stuffed them in madhouses.

One day Mr Angelcakes found a little girl who could help him and her name was Boo Boo. He decided he would make her into a warrior. And when she was old enough she would steal the butterfly and kill Hummingbird–

Suddenly Pedrock came into the room. Mr Angelcakes disappeared, popped like a balloon. A fizzle-whiff of ice-cream scent hung in the air. Sweet-stale.

I was so frightened I did not know what to say, so I said nothing. If an Angel had been speaking to me, he must have been telling me the truth, and so I shut my mouth.

Before I fell asleep I counted the wobbly stars in the sky. I counted them until my eyelids shut like a book.

And I dreamt of skin, rolls and rolls of weird fabric. And there were angels sewing human skin costumes. Black threads looped through silver-sharp needles. Soggy bits were discarded, slung aside. Scraps for the angel-dogs. They chattered amongst themselves and their language was strange: squawks and low murmurs. Squealing and tongue clicking. Is this what angels really sound like? A mishmash of other sounds. Stolen perhaps. Around my neck was a magnifying glass on a black chain. A necklace. I held it up to my eyes and peered through the peephole. I could see them for what they really were.

Rotting things, falling apart in time. Leathery bubbling skin, green popping eyeballs.

I put the magnifying glass down and hunched over and vomited by my feet.

• • •

The next evening, Prunella kicked Guardian, so I slammed her head into the trifle dish and found it surprisingly easy. I could have killed her.

Mr Angelcakes came again that very same night and he brought me an axe.

"I want you to chop Mr Icarus Hookeye's head off."

"Why?"

"It is a test. And if you refuse I will skin your brother."

I did what he said without question. I crept down into the kitchen. I could see Mr Hookeye looking out of the window. I jumped up onto the table and ran towards him, swinging the axe. He turned towards me, a look of surprise on his face, and I sliced his head off as easily as slicing a piece of cake. It bounced on the floor.

Mr Angelcakes was very happy with me. He licked my arm.

The remaining days at the Grubweed house passed like a daydream. I played in the garden with Guardian, and picked blackberries and wild flowers in the woods. I imagined there were ghosts wandering about sulking, and I waved at them. Prodded them with sticks, chased them with butterfly nets.

Mr Angelcakes told me that Professor Hummingbird had killed my Uncle Grubweed, turned him into a butterfly and squashed him between his fingers. Mr Angelcakes could see things other people could not. He knew secret things.

The butterfly he carved into my back hurt, but he said the Professor would want me if he saw it. So I stopped complaining. I shut my stupid mouth.

I dreamt that I was a black butterfly. Monstrous. Landing on poppy heads, devouring their juices. I pulsated and swirl-danced like a little demon, red eyed and hungry. Stepping into space, I hovered over the strange little earth: my body a hot engine. A great emptiness expanded within me.

I am an imploding star.

I licked everything I touched. Wet kisses, my spit honeybee sweet. My lips razor sharp.

I dream that I am a black butterfly and my name has been erased.

Mr Angelcakes' plan worked and the Professor wanted to adopt me. He took me to his castle in the woods to grow up. The forest is deep and full of giant toadstools and goblin laughter. Roots of the trees are like muscles, swelling and aching under the soil. Milk-white flowers and stingy nettles grow in handfuls round the paths. Dark, secret and happy moss spreads in moist places. If people get lost in these woods they turn into a plant. Flesh becomes vegetation.

That night, I ate jam tarts for pudding with the Professor. I was his adopted daughter. I was his special girl. I knew I would miss Guardian, but Pedrock would look after him. My bedroom was bigger than my old one and I had a big red bed, a looking glass and a box full of toy knights on horses. My favourite was the black knight, who was the biggest. I liked the colour black because it is not a colour, it is like a hole in space. I made him kill all the other knights, hack them down. Mr Angelcakes played with me; he was very pleased with me.

The Professor took a photograph of me sitting on a chair. He told me to be very still, as though I was dead. He said I was unusual. He is an expert in unusual creatures.

A puff of smoke! And the photograph was done. I was caught like a fairy in a jam jar.

I explored my new home. Found all the magic rooms. I found the room with the photographs of his princesses. There are six and I am number seven. I looked at all their faces. Not one of them was pretty and yet in fairytales isn't the princess supposed to be beautiful? Aren't they supposed to be delicate, beautiful things? We are his butterfly girls. Seven of us stuck on the wall, trapped beneath glass.

Caught

Last night Detective White tried to rescue me. Maybe Detective White is a prince? He stuffed me through a window and told me to run. Mr Loveheart blew up part of the Professor's house. Mr Angelcakes thought that was really funny. Mr Angelcakes says he really likes Mr Loveheart, he says he is a *Wild Card*. I ask what a *Wild Card* is and Mr Angelcakes says, "**Unpredictable, anything could happen.**" Mr Loveheart has black eyes like an insect, but he isn't one.

He's glittery, sparkling, candles on a birthday cake. He's only for special occasions.

Detective White, Mr Loveheart and Constable Walnut have all disappeared. Mr Angelcakes says they are on the wall in a frame. They have become butterflies. I am sorry for it.

• • •

It is a week later and Mr Angelcakes has given me some chalk, and tells me to draw butterflies in the courtyard, as many as possible because the Professor will like it very much. And so I do, I begin my wonky butterfly drawings, some with enormous leaf-like wings; some squint and limp looking; some soaring like dragons, heavy and hell-raisers. I hear a clippety-clop and a pony and trap arrive and out steps a man called Detective Waxford. He looks very angry and he shouts at the Professor and takes us both to London. I sit in his office and draw butterflies on his desk with the chalk. He asks me questions and I tell him what I know. He thinks I am mad.

The Professor's lawyer, Mr Evening-Star, says that we are both free to go and that Detective Waxford has no evidence. Mr Evening-Star has a face like an eel: greyish skin stretched over his skull.

We return home and I am so tired I fell asleep on the train and the Professor has to carry me to bed.

For the next ten or twenty years, or so it seems to me, I grow up in the home of the Professor, the moated castle in the forest. Am I in a fairytale? All the dresses I have are black. It is the only colour he wants me to wear, yet it is not a colour. I am not allowed to see anyone. I must remain in the castle but I am allowed to wander into the woods, as long as I don't stray too far. Sometimes I think I can hear Guardian howling, but I know he is well loved and very well fed and so I am not sad. Pedrock will cuddle him all the time. I imagine I am a strange queen under a terrible curse. I imagine I am a butterfly trapped under glass. I imagine I am the Professor's wife.

During the days I wander into the woods and play games in my head, pick flowers, chase ghosts and fight with a wooden sword the Professor gave me. I hack away at the trees. I cleave great chunks out of them. I am trying to disguise how strong I am becoming.

At night Mr Angelcakes blindfolds me. He says I must learn to be able to fight without seeing. I must pretend I am blind. I can't do it at first. I stumble around, smack my head on the wall, stub my toe. And then he tells me to focus, to think about the Professor's favourite butterfly. I see it inside my head, all the black and red, the huge wings and then the slow, slow beating of wings. I look into the eyes on the wings, they see all. Time is slowing down. I can see everything without opening my eyes.

Now I fight in the woods with my blindfold on. I CHOP CHOP CHOP.

I CHOP CHOP CHOP the air.

I think about the butterfly. It is swimming in my head. It is lighting fast. CHOP CHOP CHOP.

I dismember space.

I need something better to practice on.

I need a real weapon.

I have turned eight years old. The Professor gives me a present. It is a black heart pendant. He puts it on my neck. He says, "Never take it off, Boo Boo," and so I obey him. I wonder what colour my heart is? I wonder if, it too is black. I touch the space in my chest and feel for a beat.

THUD THUD THUD

How fast does a butterfly's heart beat ?

We are having a guest for dinner tonight. His name is Sebastian Crabmouth. He is a medical doctor and the Professor has known him for many years.

Mr Angelcakes would like me to kill him over dinner.

The three of us sit round the dinner table. Tonight we are eating roast duck with plums and buttered potatoes. For pudding there is a birthday cake the Professor bought in a London cake shop. It is red with vanilla sponge and a cream filling. Sebastian

Crabmouth is a little man with dark hair and spectacles, and a round squashy face. I look at my knife and fork and I think about murder. I know Mr Angelcakes will want to be amused.

"Happy birthday, Boo Boo. The Professor tells me you are eight today," says Mr Crabmouth.

"Do you collect butterflies too?" I ask.

"No, I am the Professor's physician and I also run a practice in London."

How long, I wonder, do I have to wait before I can kill him?

The Professor turns to Mr Crabmouth. "Sebastian, I was thinking of inviting the explorer Oberon Lionheart over for dinner one evening. I hear he has some specimens of the emperor moth and I would love to arrange an exhibition."

I throw my fork at Mr Crabmouth's head. It sinks between his eyes, buried deep in his skull. He dies instantly.

The Professor stares at me with interest. "Boo Boo, dear. That was a bad thing you just did."

"But you won't tell me off, will you, because you want to marry me?"

The birthday cake tastes delicious.

Mr Angelcakes is very pleased with me. But I feel I need more practice. More human targets. But no

one comes to visit and so I have no one I can kill.
  Boo.
  Hoo.

Dream of the Angel-Eater

It is the witching hour when the Angel-Eater comes to me. Floats above my bed. Speaks to me directly.

She is a great black star.

"Our souls are under glass squashed together. You must get someone to break us out!" she says, hovering over me.

"Where are you?" I stand on my bed.

"On your wedding night he will reveal me. It is his pattern. You have to wait."

POP

She vanishes into the wallpaper.

I dream of edible clocks. Each one tastes like insect-meat.

London
THE BUTTERFLY EXHIBITION

I am nine years old and I have had to wait a whole year but target practice has finally come. Tonight the Professor is taking me to an exhibition in London at the British Museum. The famous explorer, Oberon Lionheart, will be there with his moths. Mr Angelcakes has given me two butterfly blades made from silver. They slot neatly down my high leather-laced boots. The Professor looks at me quizzically. "Are you going to kill anyone tonight, dearest?"

"Very likely," I say.

"Can I ask you to refrain from murdering Mr Lionheart, at least until I get to quiz him on his emperors?"

A huge banner hangs outside the steps to the British Museum with the emperor moth, in all its dazzling blues and purples. It is very beautiful, but not as rare as the Professor's. Mr Angelcakes tells me to kill as many people as possible. So I will try my best.

I am let loose to roam free in the exhibition, and I would say there's about fifty people here and a large amount of champagne. I take a glass and try it, the bubbles fizz up my nose. There are also strawberries and cream, big bowls of them. I dip my fingers in the cream. It's like a bowl full of angel tears, delicious.

I see a huge man with a mane of red gold hair and great bushy beard. He must be the famous explorer, Lionheart. I go up and say hello.

"My name is Boo Boo. I am Professor Hummingbird's adopted daughter."

"Well, well," he growls. "It's an honour to meet you little miss," and he shakes my hand with his great paw. "And what do you think of my emperors?" He points a finger behind him to where a row of them sit encased in a display cabinet, each one a deep midnight purple blue. Like the eyes of mermaids.

"They are very beautiful, Mr Lionheart. Have you seen the Professor's angel-eater?"

Mr Lionheart is startled. "I had no idea he possessed one."

"Oh yes, he hangs it usually in his bedroom, or the study, if guests are coming to visit. Maybe you will come and see us?"

"I would love to Miss Boo Boo," and he smiles a great predatory smile. I like him very much. I have decided not to kill him.

I amble lazily up the stairs with a handful of strawberries which I am popping into my mouth, as if I was a god eating severed heads. I can see the Professor now talking with Mr Lionheart.

I wait.

I am approached by a gentleman with a fuzzy red moustache and a cigar in one hand.

"Hello, my dear. My name is Rufus Hazard."

"Hello," I reply. "Are you a collector of butter-flies?"

"Egad, no! I'm an adventurer, my little one. A thrill seeker, treasure hunter. Most recently I had my leg chewed by an amorous witch."

"Why was she chewing your leg?"

"Animal magnetism. I'm a dangerous chap around the women." His upper lip wobbles.

"They can't seem to control themselves around me. You're too young to understand my dear. But let me tell you, I'm cursed with a terrible affliction."

"Delusion?"

"No," he continues unabashed. "Sexual magnetism."

I actually feel sorry for him so I fling him out of the window. He screams and lands safely in a dust cart ambling off into the shadows.

"What the blazes?" he yells.

I remove the blades from my boots and extend them as if they were wings.

It is like a dance. I can feel the limbs fly off as I spin. I can hear the screaming and the running. I can smell them: it's sweat, human shit and semen. Fear between their legs; in their throats vomit. Heads spin off my blades. It's a beautiful dance. I can see the butterfly in my head, I can hear Mr Angelcakes laughing and clapping. Chop chop, spin spin.

Chop

    chop

        chop.

Silence. I am standing in a heap of body parts. The Professor is watching me from the corner of the room, eyes like dark pools. He's excited by me but he also fears me.

He takes the emperor moths and we get into the coach and drive back home. Into the darkness; into the deep, beautiful darkness.

Fourteen

That is how old I am. I have an insatiable desire to kill. It's like a fever running inside me. I lie on my bed and put my hands between my legs.

Mr Angelcakes says I have surpassed what he thought was possible. He runs his finger up and down my thigh. The skin suit he is wearing is beginning to rot. I have sucked so much power out of him. He is just a voice now and a sack of skin. But I follow his commands. I am stronger than Mr Angelcakes. I am stronger than the Professor. Why don't I kill them both? Because then I will be alone.

Mr Angelcakes speaks to me, his rotting green tongue lolling inside his mouth. **"My little weapon."** He strokes my face.

I am going mad.

Melting into the floorboards.

Pedrock grows up, 1899
SAILING

The lake today is full of silvery threads and spirals of colour. Insects dart over the surface, deeply in love with their reflections. I have returned to the village of Darkwound and borrowed Grandpa's boat. I have returned for my little sister's wedding. I haven't seen her in ten years. He has kept her locked away. The little boat glides gently over the water, like a leaf. Gliding without any particular purpose. I can see the edge of the woods, the edge of the world.

I work as a clerk in the ship-building firm of Winkhood & Son in London, and have lodgings near St Martin's. I am courting a hat maker's daughter, a Miss Penny Seashell, with hair the colour of white honeycomb beaches and eyes as green as algae.

Much has happened over the last ten years. Mrs Charm's Medieval Horrors were published and a phenomenal success; she is currently writing her seventh book, *The Wicked Monk of Winchester*, which again explores the notion of demonic possession in the clergy. I have read and enjoyed them all. She misses Mr Loveheart terribly and dedicates all her books to him, hoping secretly that he is somewhere safe, reading them, and not dead as everyone believes. Cornelius, who is now twenty-six, has sadly become an opium addict and is cared for by his mother at home. He has also become fascinated with turnips, which, I have been informed by the village apothecary, Mr Pinhole, is a side effect of the drug usage, although Mrs Charm tells me this is complete nonsense and Mr Pinhole has been obviously self-prescribing himself laudanum. Grandpa is still with us, at the ripe age of ninety, but Guardian the dog died after a night of howling at Boo Boo's window and is buried under a rose bush in the garden. His ghost, I am sure, watches over her. He will forever be her Guardian.

Prunella and Estelle, now twenty, are plump, pretty and blonde, with the sole intention of marrying Horatio Beetle, who is still unmarried, although has broken a string of hearts according to village gossip, and has by all accounts several bastard children in the village. Mr Grubweed was never found and Mrs Grubweed has still not yet uttered a word. Whether she has chosen never to speak or is simply unable to remains a mystery.

Mr Wormhole, the vicar, will be performing the wedding service for my sister next Saturday. He remains still paranoid that he will join the other "missing".

The sun is starting to set, an orange ball sinking; the moon, as white as baby teeth, emerging. My little boat floats on under this new moonlight, sweaty glinting water ripples. It moves forward, it must keep moving forward.

Above in the black sky, a comet tail blazes and explodes. Ribbons of gold and shocking phosphorescence dazzle. It is the most beautiful thing I have ever seen, and yet it is

the

death

of

a

star.

The butterflies in the house
of Hummingbird
are shaking on the walls.
The glass
is cracking

Ten years. Ten bloody years. White and Walnut pop into my head every day. Even the mad Mr Loveheart! I couldn't find you, I am so sorry, I couldn't find you. I dream of butterflies. They dance behind my eyes, soar in my brain. I am infested by them.

I sink back into my chair, peek at a file on a local strangler. Sip my tea, plop another sugar lump in and give it a swirl. Mrs Sultana, the tea lady, wheels her trolley in and gives me a sticky bun.

"Cheer up, ducky," she says.

"Thank you Mrs Sultana," I grumble in reply.

She squeaks her trolley off and I hear her in the corridor, "He's such a big grumpy pussy cat."

Constable Luck peeks his head round the door.

"Sir, there's a gentleman here to see you. Says he has information on Professor Hummingbird."

My brain wakes up, "Send him in, and get some more tea and buns off the trolley would you."

"Yes, sir."

A moment later a large black bearded man enters my office looking extremely uncomfortable.

"I am Detective Waxford. Please take seat Mr…?"

"Otto Ink-Squid," he says, and he does, squashing himself into the wobbly chair.

Constable Luck appears and plops a mug of tea on the table and a plate of buns and retreats.

"So, what do want to tell me, Mr Ink-Squid?"

"I have some worrying information regarding this wedding announcement," and he plops a copy of today's *Times* on my desk and points to the newspaper article:

ANNOUNCEMENT

Professor Gabriel Hummingbird, the eminent anthropologist, is to marry Miss Boo Boo Frogwish on August 8th at St Cuthbert's Church in the village of Darkwound, Kent.

My heart is full of butterflies. They pound within my chest. "Go on," and I await his answer.

"It is something quite disturbing. I must tell you quite a story. I own a magic emporium in Spitalfields. I have had the business for over twenty years. Ten years ago a girl came into my shop for help. Professor Hummingbird had buried her alive."

I see a butterfly on the window flutter past.

Mr Ink-Squid's voice is full of sadness. "My shop is located on Beeswax Lane: I sell Ouija boards, Psychic Trays and tarot cards; that sort of thing. I don't get many customers, mostly postal orders from a very peculiar cliental. So, I was quite shocked when she fell through my front door, covered in mud and in her night gown. Bare feet, hysterical. I told her to sit down, got her a blanket and a cup of tea. I tried to calm her down. She told me her name was Guinevere Harlowe and she was sixteen years old. She said she was the wife of a Professor Hummingbird, a marriage arranged by her father, whom she described as a famous collector of butterflies and moths. She told me her family had a large collection of fine specimens: ghost moths, from Peru, 'worth a fortune to an avid collector,' she said. She told me that was what Professor Hummingbird had wanted. That was what he was after."

Mr Ink-Squid paused and drank some tea. He looked weary. He felt like me. He felt the weight of a world gone mad.

"Please continue, Mr Ink-Squid," I said gently

"She told me about the wedding night. She said he was–" he paused,"–there was something abnormal about his desires."

I waited.

"She said the morning after the wedding, a funeral carriage arrived. She asked him 'Who is dead? Who has died?' He had replied, 'Why you of course, my dear.'"

I waited.

"He's a monster," Mr Ink-Squid shuddered. "A deranged collector. She told me she was screaming, tried to run, but they caught her, the Professor and his vile brother, Ignatius. Caught her, drugged her and stuffed her in a coffin. She said she awoke in darkness. Running out of air. She said she was dying."

"How did she escape?" I leant forward

"A boy dug her up, opened the coffin. She said she would have thought him an angel, but he looked sinister. Said he had eyes as black as nightmares. Reminded her of a little shark. He opened the coffin lid and said to her, 'Do not go back to your husband, as he will kill you. Do not return to your father, for he is murdered. Seek help from a man called Otto Ink-Squid who runs an emporium on Beeswax Lane.'"

"That is most queer," I said taking another sticky bun.

"Yes, apparently he said he had saved her because he objected to people being buried who are not actually dead. Well, she pulled herself out quick as she could and made her way to my little shop. I have no idea who this young boy is and why he would have recommended me to her aid."

"And she didn't go to the police?"

"No, she was terrified, as she was still his wife and property. He would have killed her. I said that she could stay with me until we could sort something out. She had no family: her monies were in the possession of that villain, Hummingbird. She stayed with me for three months and eventually I arranged her transportation to Paris to stay with my sister; to begin a new life. I gave her the money to do it and she never came back. She is now engaged to a Captain Flint of the British navy, who knows nothing of her past, and will travel with him to the South Americas. When I read the article of his young girl's forthcoming marriage, well, I had to try to prevent it somehow."

"Would Guinevere Harlowe be prepared to make a statement?"

"I cannot have her involved in this. If he knew she were alive he would surely try to murder her."

"I cannot arrest a man on a mere rumour. I need her statement; I need proof, Mr Ink-Squid."

"She does not know I have come here. I vowed I would never betray her trust. But seeing this young girl is to be married to him. It is a death sentence."

"This young girl, Boo Boo, will be his seventh wife," I say and lean back into my chair, thinking.

"Seventh?" Mr Ink-Squid cries. "There must be something that can be done. There must be!"

"Tell me, Mr Ink-Squid, do you believe in fate? You do run a magic emporium, so I expect you are predisposed towards the more unusual and unexplained aspects of life?"

"Well, yes, I suppose. It was my father's shop originally. He was a magician, performed on stage, and when he retired opened the shop. It's all illusion, of course: hidden mirrors, sleight of hand."

"Yes, illusion, quite. I have met this girl Boo Boo before. She was his adopted daughter. My friend Detective White went missing at the Professor's house while trying to rescue her."

"I am so sorry. Do you believe him murdered?" he replies

"I have never found out the truth. The only witness was the girl and do you know what she said to me?"

I pause.

"She said he had turned him into a butterfly."

"Perhaps she was in shock?" he said

"That's what I thought for many years. It has haunted me. I cannot let it go and yet there have been no further developments. I keep dreaming about that girl and what she said."

"It is guilt, perhaps. It weighs heavily on your mind. He was your friend."

"What if she was telling the truth?"

"It is an impossible thing you suggest. Maybe you should speak to her again, convince her not to marry this monster. Maybe she will remember what really happened."

"Thank you, Mr Ink-Squid, for your information. I will see what I can do and I will keep you informed if there are any developments," and I shake his hand.

"I would be most grateful. We cannot let anything happen to that young woman," and he leaves me sinking into my chair; the weight of darkness pressing upon me.

I suddenly remember seeing a magician's trick of

concealing a butterfly in his top hat so it flew out. It escaped only at the end.

This bloody place never changes! Deranged woodlands, crawling with specimens of toadstools with fangs and potato-brained villagers.

I am outside the home of Professor Hummingbird. I know that he is away on business in London, seeing his brother Ignatius. I knock on the door. If no one replies I will break in.

A young woman in a black dress opens the door.

"Ah, Miss Boo Boo. Hello again. It has been many years since we last met."

"I remember you," she says.

"I need to ask you once again, what happened to Detective White, Constable Walnut and Mr Loveheart?"

"Please, come in," she says, and I follow her into the hall of red and she points to three butterflies on the wall: one brown, one white and one bright red.

"It is as I told you before. The Professor turned them into butterflies."

"You realise what you are telling me is madness."

She doesn't respond. She is a very strange young woman, moving silently, as though she does not exist.

"I need to know what happened to them. I have to know."

"I have already told you."

"*Are they alive?*" I shout, gripping her by the shoulders. She doesn't flinch.

"Yes, but they are trapped."

"What must I do to free them?"

"Smash the glass," she says, so softly.

"What?" I say, almost laughing. "You have gone mad!"

"Smash the glass," she says again, willing me to do it.

"*Lunacy!*" I shout.

"Smash the glass," she says again.

I pick up the butterflies and smash the frame against the wall. The glass smashes into pieces. I can hear lightning crack in the sky and a hand touches my shoulder. I turn round and Mr Loveheart is smiling at me. "Detective Waxford. I am making a confession in advance. I am going put the Professor's head on a stick outside Scotland Yard and then blow his house up... again."

"Loveheart?" I am confounded. Detective White and Constable Walnut are standing beside him.

"You look older, Waxford," Detective White says, rather wobbly on his feet. "It must be this case getting to you."

"Thank God, you're alive." I am nearly crying with disbelief.

I turn to the girl. "You could have freed them. Why didn't you?"

"I can't. I am a butterfly." And she wanders off down the hallway.

"Now, she *is* interesting," remarks Loveheart.

"We have to stop the wedding," I blurt out.

"What wedding?" says Detective White.

"You've all been trapped for ten years. It's 1899. That girl is Boo Boo, and the Professor is marrying her next Saturday."

"My grandma is going to be rather worried," say Constable Walnut.

"I wouldn't concern yourself, Walnut," replies Loveheart. "She already thinks you're dead."

"What on earth do I tell her?"

"Say you were on a sabbatical."

"For ten years?"

"Coma?"

"She's not buying that. I need something more convincing."

"Bullet in the brain… amnesia."

"Shut up the pair of you," says Detective White. "There is proof, Waxford, against Hummingbird." And Detective White shows me the room where the photographs of his wives are hanging.

The glass cracks.

BONG!
BONG!
BONG!

BIG BEN GOES BACKWARDS.

10 YEARS fall off the clock.

The perils of using Black Magic!
The spell is broken
The glass is broken
TIME IS BROKEN
THE YEAR IS BACK TO 1889
And yet, we are still the same.

Death wakes up from a snooze, checks his pocket watch, and sighs.

1889, *again!*
MR LOVEHEART & THE WOOING
OF BOO BOO

I've decided I shall marry her! She's perfect for me. We go together like cheese and pickle (am I the pickle, perhaps?). Of course I shall have to murder her fiancé but I can't suppose anyone will mind too much; he's an insane insect collector. He's only after your wings, Boo Boo!

Loveheart Manor has become rather overgrown after ten years. I have to hack my way through thorny shrubs and teethy rose bushes with my sword. Ouch! This reminds me of a fairytale. Now which one is it?

Hack, hack, hack!

My gardens are wild. A fleshy patchwork quilt of fruit, weed and flowers. They burst at the touch; shape into hearts and break within my hands. My kingdom, my beautiful kingdom.

A big orange cat is sitting on my front steps; his bottom a splatty shape. "And I shall name you 'Pumpkin'," I say, "because you resemble one."

The cat looks at me with disgust, his jade eyes narrowing, and then raises his tail and breaks wind.

"That's not very nice, is it, Pumpkin?" Naughty cat. And he won't budge from my front step. He's blocking the door with his huge shape. I wonder what he's been eating? Possibly my neighbours.

I shall have to climb through a window. "Pumpkin, you must guard the entrance to my kingdom."

The cat yawns.

"I am the Lord of the Underworld," I explain.

He isn't impressed. Well, that's cats for you.

I leap through a downstairs window into my library. Bit dusty in here. Cough. Splutter. I am looking for some rose shears. I have decided to collect some flowers for Boo Boo. My insect queen. I sprint into the kitchens and Ah Yes! GARDENING shears, underneath the sink perhaps? No. Oh well, I shall use my sword instead.

Mr Fingers floats in the mirror in the hallway. A specimen in a jar. He doesn't appear to be able to die. Dizzy in the eyes; full of stars. I tap on the glass. He stirs like a baby in a womb. Bares his teeth. Mad dog.

I should end this. This has gone on too long.

"Goodbye, Mr Fingers," I say.

I drive my sword through the mirror and it smashes. An explosion of glass, a scream. He disintegrates. The house shakes. My kingdom wakes. The Underworld is awake. Tentacles of black break through the earth in my kingdom and coil into my trees, they wind themselves about the flowers and into the architecture of my house.

I open the front door. Pumpkin the cat is unaffected by the huge disturbance of undergrowth. The landscape is shifting, distorted. My rose bushes are blooming; the roses so red they stab my eyes. Big bloody petals intoxicate and overpower all other flowers.

My crown sits on the hall table, glinting. I pop it on my head. Glitter magic thing. Dark star. Best keep it on from now.

A dark fairy zooms past in the hedgerow and Pumpkin the cat moves like an arrow after it, his enormous bottom wobbling off into the wilderness.

I step into my gardens with my sword and start collecting roses for my beloved Boo Boo. My queen of hearts.

The under-stink of this new world is a little like meat being left out too long. It merges within my kingdom of hearts, invents new plants, new life forms. I may have problems finding a gardener.

An armful of roses: they are big girls, heavy petals, red as meat; thorns like fairy blades. I shall gather her a mountain of them. A bloody wobbly tower of them with perhaps a little note attached.

Would you like to be my queen and live in my Palace of Hearts?

A heart in every room, on everything (including the chamber pots), and all of them for you, my love. Every one for you.

I find magpie feathers on the path and a coil of snail shells. Wonderful things, little parts of my garden. The language of fairies: magic gobbledygook floats in my kingdom. And now a staircase coiling to the underworlds has appeared. Coiling down into dark places; black feathers and toad croak. I leave the roses in a powerful heap by my door and go down the staircase to inspect my other kingdom. Pumpkin the cat watches me from a distance, licking his paws. What did the fairy taste like, I wonder?

A loopy amputation – that is what it feels like to walk down into the underworlds. You'll feel disembowelled, stepping into deep magic. The Kingdom of the Underworld adjusts itself to its ruler.

Before, under the rule of Mr Fingers, it was made of demented clockwork; the constant ticking of mechanical contraptions; the sounds of time. Regulated, obsessive tinkering.

I step into a world now of black hearts: jam flowers, fairies with tartan slippers, a river of red flower petals. Lush, nervous energy, bursting fairytales. The clocks have melted. Time has no meaning here anymore. My world is an upside down fairytale. A heart lollipop on a stick. Go on, give me a lick.

A little madness never hurt anyone.

I wander amongst my Palace of Hearts. I am alone here, despite the wildlife. I have no queen. No heirs. There is of course Pumpkin the cat, he would make a very fine ruler of the Underworlds.

Death appears. "Don't you dare!"

"Dare what?" I turn around, surprised. He always pops up at the strangest moments.

"Don't bequeath your new kingdom to an overweight cat." He examines the lollipops. "This is an improvement from last time, if a little peculiar."

"I didn't know you could read my thoughts."

"Sometimes, and it's quite unnerving. You will be wondering what your responsibilities are now, I suppose. Mr Fingers spent most of his time collecting assassin sons and clocks. You will serve a greater purpose, I hope," and he eyes me rather sternly.

"Shall we have some tea and cake?" I motion him towards a table under a black tree of raspberry jelly heads. Eyes made of marshmallows. On the table sits a pot of steaming tea and a plate of chocolate éclairs. Death pours the tea and adds three lumps of sugar and a dash of milk.

"You're looking very well," I say, for the sake of polite conversation.

His eyes turn from a deep shade of gold to black and fix upon me. His hand selects an éclair.

"Now then. I will be keeping an eye on you, Mr Loveheart. You can be rather naughty and unpredictable."

I take my pistol out and shoot something above his head, which screams and falls to the ground with a thud.

"As I was saying," continues Death, completely unfazed, "You can see this underworld is organic. It moulds itself to its king. Shapeshifts around you. You have made it bloom with life, Mr Loveheart, burst with it. It was a stagnant, dark place before. Now it is energy. It fizzes."

A fairy with indigo wings zooms round Death's head. Sits on his shoulder. She's after his éclair.

"Another lump?" I pass him the sugar bowl.

"No, thank you," and he peers at the fairy, who refuses to move from his shoulder. She squeaks some instructions at him.

"Your creatures are as impertinent as you are!" and he passes her an éclair. She picks it up, (it's the same size as her) and carries it off.

"I'm very fond of fairies. They bite, you know, if you don't give them sugar."

Death eats his éclair. "This is very tasty. I see you're thinking of wooing Miss Boo Boo."

"Yes."

"Professor Hummingbird is in the way of course. He will have to be removed," says Death.

"Why *do* you help me?"

"Because I like you, Mr Loveheart. And because, I too am lonely."

Pumpkin the cat mews from the top of the staircase at Loveheart Manor. He wants an eclair.

Revenge is best served with custard

I am sitting in my office, eating a custard tart.

It's Monday morning and surprisingly chilly. I am looking at the *Times*, who have printed on their front page all six photographs of every wife of the Professor's. Their faces stare out of the pages like fish underwater.

MURDER INVESTIGATION

Urgent information required on the identity and whereabouts of these missing women, all previous wives of the anthropologist, Professor Gabriel Hummingbird, brother of Ignatius Hummingbird. Scotland Yard are investigating.

I eat the ooze, lick the pastry clean.

Boo Boo
SIXTEEN

I am engaged to be married to the Professor. The wedding is next week. I examine myself in my looking glass and touch the black heart round my throat. Am I uninteresting, ugly, wretched? Am I a lunatic, gone mad, a killing machine? Am I a pretty girl, beautiful girl? None of these things, all of these things. What am I? Butterfly, butterfly, butterfly, butterfly, butterfly.

I think about the Angel-Eater, the tattoo on my back. I am marked with her, she is part of me. Under my skin, inside my bones. Black wings, sharp as a razor edge. Slice me up with your love; dissect me. Open me up and find butterflies inside my stomach,

Today the Professor is in London on business. More butterflies to capture. I wander round the house. My head is full of prisons, vaults, hidden chambers, locked windows and doors. I keep hearing a beating of wings. Mr Angelcakes sleeps next to me every night but he says things will change after the wedding. I must kill the Professor and take the butterfly and then Mr Angelcakes will lick my skin with a thousand green-tongued kisses.

I cannot kill him yet. He has my soul under glass.

Today Detective Waxford arrives. I tell him where Detective White is. Finally he smashes the frame and sets them free. Mr Loveheart looks at me strangely. His eyes follow me about like a puppy dog. Does he know what I am? My black dress slips like trickling black waters along the courtyard. He follows me outside into the warmth.

"You are engaged to be married? You've not picked well, Miss Boo Boo. He's a bit of a shit."

"Who would you rather I married, Mr Loveheart?"

"I was hoping we could get to know each other a little better. You're very compelling."

"Your timing is terrible."

He steps closer. "Really?"

I throw him in the moat.

Night-Time Fizz

Puffs of black magic. Sleepy time.

    My

           head

                 is a

                          spoon.

You fill me with jam.

The Angel-Eater. Wings beating above me.

My spooky sister.

"Hello again," I say. My words are bubbles; they make pops.

Black flutter. Insect judder. Flippety flap.

Give me some sugar.
Make me your cake.

I dream of butterflies, I dream of butter.

I dream of butterflies.

I dream of butter.

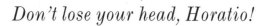
Don't lose your head, Horatio!

The Beetles have invited me for afternoon tea. Repugnant things! Slippery black, slime tongued socialites. It is Wednesday. It is three days before my wedding. The Professor is still away in London, staying with his brother; perhaps a bachelor party? He will not return until the Saturday. So I must entertain myself as best I can. Mr Angelcakes and I play hide and seek. He smells so bad, I find him easily in the pantry, small pieces of rotten greenish black flesh falling from him.

"You need new skin, Mr Angelcakes."

"**When you kill the Professor I will be strong** again. Perhaps I will wear his skin."

The gloom dark of the pantry makes his eyes glint putrid yellow.

"**Go and play with the beetles. Squash them.**"

He smiles with what is left of his lips.

I wear my long black velvet dress. Only ever black for the Professor. He doesn't explain his preferences, he just expects conformity.

The Beetle mansion, cream coloured and orderly. A nice neat green lawn. A perfectly acceptable border of flowers, neatly positioned, controllable.

Lady Beetle and her son sit wearing a dark shade of purple in their garden. A tea pot and tea cups neatly arranged before them. A pile of delicate sandwiches and fairy-like cakes. Beetle, I think. Beetle, rolling dung, living in shit.

"Good afternoon, Miss Frogwish," says Lady Beetle, dryly. She is wondering how far up the society ladder I will climb once I become Mrs Hummingbird.

"Good afternoon," I reply and sit down beside Horatio Beetle, now twenty-six years old, dashingly handsome and still a nasty little boy. He is watching me playfully.

"You interest me, Boo Boo." He wants to play games with me. "Your eyes are mischievous, trying to bewitch me. I am, as you may have heard, a heart-breaker. I leave a trail of weeping women in my wake. Much like Lord Byron, I am *mad, bad and dangerous to know.*"

"What a fucking pile of shit," I say and remove my butterfly blades from my boots. "You're an ignorant child and I am going to teach you a lesson in manners to women."

I slice off his mother's head first and fling it aside. He has defecated himself like an animal and is crawling away from me screaming. I throw both blades, which land in his eyes, impaling him to the ground. I cut off his head and fling it in the pond.

This is too easy. I am bored with this.

Mr Loveheart appears, sprinting across the lawn with a bunch of roses. He bows very low. "I thought you dealt with them rather tastefully." He hands me the flowers.

"I am not available, Mr Loveheart. I am getting married on Saturday."

"Then I will have to kill your wretched fiancé in a duel."

"Duel? You were intent on blowing him up."

"Yes, because it's funnier. Miss Frogwish, my heart is in your hands, dear lady."

"You have very pretty eyes, Mr Loveheart."

"I won't let you marry him, Boo Boo. I will not give up on you."

I take the flowers and walk through the woods and think about his eyes, which are black like mine.

Detectives Waxford and White find Pandora

I am outside the Lupine Asylum with Detective White. We have found Pandora, the fourth wife of Professor Hummingbird, committed to the madhouse. Of his six wives, we have discovered through advertisement in the *Times* that three are dead, one was buried alive and now lives in Paris and two were committed to an asylum, one escaping with the help of Mr Loveheart. This is our last lady.

Pandora is outside in the courtyard on a seat, knitting. It appears to be an extraordinary long yellow scarf she is making, despite there being a heatwave.

"Hello, Pandora. My name is Detective Waxford and this is Detective White. We would like to ask you some questions regarding your late husband, Professor Gabriel Hummingbird. He will be marrying a sixteen year-old girl this Saturday."

She looks up from her knitting. The scarf, I estimate, must be twenty foot long, at least.

"Is she pretty?" Pandora asks, her voice very light and childlike.

"She is sixteen, madam, and in danger," I say.

"He said I was pretty," sighs Pandora. "He said that before we got married. Afterwards, he just said I was insane."

"What happened to you? How did you end up here?"

Pandora continues to knit, the great heaps of butter yellow wool trailing like Rapunzel's hair by her feet. "After the wedding night, he seemed bored with me already. I didn't know how to please him. Maybe I should have made him a cake with some sugared flowers or a meringue. I'm not mad. I am a good girl. I am a good girl."

I think to myself, she has been driven mad. He may as well have killed her.

Detective White kneels by her side. "It is a very beautiful scarf," he says kindly.

"Thank you. The fairies helped me."

Detective White and I head back to Scotland Yard. We are being followed.

"Percival, there's something watching us," I say, and glance over my shoulder, catching sight of a top-hatted gentleman with an eye patch. Instead of flinching, he acknowledges my suspicions with amusement.

When we arrive at Scotland Yard, Constable Walnut is waiting for us by the entrance, eating a mutton pie.

"Detectives, there's a lady here to see you." He looked at me sheepishly, wiping crumbs from his lips.

"Thank you, Walnut." I open the door to my office. A lady in a long, moth-grey veil which covers her face is perched nervously on a chair by my desk.

"Good morning," I say.

"Are you Henry Waxford?" her voice nervous, her small hand in a lace glove, pointing at me. She looks as though she belongs in another world, like a little ghost.

"Yes, and this is my colleague, Detective White. How may we help you madam?"

"I saw the pictures of those poor women in the *Times*. The brides of Gabriel Hummingbird. How many are still alive?"

"Three. Would you like some tea, Miss…?"

"Yes please. My name is Mary Summerfly."

I pop my head out of the door and ask Walnut to bring in some tea and biscuits.

"Did you know any of these women?" I ask, sitting myself back down again.

"No, I never met any of them. I... I am..." She struggles terribly with the words.

"Are you alright, miss?" asks Detective White.

"No, I am not. My life is in danger. I need your help. I need your protection," she gasps.

"You are safe with us, Miss Summerfly. Please tell us what has happened."

"Do you know Gabriel Hummingbird?" I interject.

"No, but I knew of his brother, Ignatius. I was brought up on the Romney Marsh. I lived with my Aunt in a small cottage near his family home. I used to take walks on the marshland and sometimes I would bump into him and we would have conversations. We would talk about the wildlife, mostly the butterflies. He seemed like an interesting, well-educated gentleman. I believe he works for the government, holds a position in the House of Lords."

Walnut enters the room, announces, "We're out of custard creams!" and lays the tray on the table.

"Thank you, Walnut," replies Detective White. He begins pouring the tea.

"Please continue," I say to her.

"A few months ago, we met up on the marshlands again. He invited me to take tea with him at his home. He said the local vicar would be there, as they would be discussing an archaeological dig to take place on the marshes. He went into some depth about the burial mound of an Anglo Saxon king. Apparently artefacts had been discovered which had caused some excitement amongst both the locals and an expert from the British Museum. I accepted his invitation and walked back with him to his house."

She suddenly goes very quiet. Detective White passes her a cup of tea. She removes her veil, revealing her face, which is ghostly white. Around her neck is a thick black choker with an ivory cameo. She sips some of the tea, her hands shaking.

"What happened, Miss Summerfly?" I ask.

"When I was inside his house he hit me across the face and I must have become unconscious. When I woke up I was in a small cage in a cellar."

Walnut steps back into the room, "I've found some hobnobs," and places them on the table.

Detective White stares at him rather seriously and he slips quietly out of the room.

"After a while two men came. They made me

drink something sweet. It made me feel sleepy. A bag was put over my head and I was dragged into a carriage and we travelled for several hours. When the carriage finally stopped I was dragged out and I heard a man say the word *butterfly*. They took me into a building and put me into another cage. The bag was taken off my head."

"What did you see?"

"Other women in cages. We were in some sort of underground cellar. Stone walls; it was very dark, a few candles burning. The ceiling had... The ceiling." She bursts into tears.

"What about the ceiling?" I persist.

"It had blood dripping from it," she sobs. "I was so frightened but I couldn't shout out, the drug... the words... No noise came from my mouth. I tried to speak to the other women. I couldn't."

"How many other woman were there?"

"Maybe ten, maybe more."

"What happened next?"

"The drug was beginning to wear off. Men came in and started opening the cages and dragging the women out. My cage was opened but before I was pulled out there was a terrible screaming, a woman started attacking one of the men, punching and kicking him. I took a chance. I ran as fast as I could, past the cages and up some stairs. I could hear them behind me. There were so many corridors, so many doors, all locked. I just kept running until I came to a door I was able to open which I burst through into the light. There were lots of men smoking and drinking and laughing. It looked like a formal club of some sort. I saw Ignatius smoking a cigar. He was just staring at me. I think he was amused. My only thought was of survival. I saw a great window on the other side of the room and I ran towards it and threw myself through it. I fell a great height into dark water. Into the Thames."

The tea cup trembled in her hands

"I thought I was going to die. I woke up washed up on the shoreline near a boatyard. I have been in hiding in lodgings in London ever since. I had been too frightened to come to you and then I saw the pictures of the women in the *Times* and I thought about all those women I left behind. God knows what happened to them." She bends her head very low.

"You are a very brave woman, Miss Summerfly, and you are under our protection now. The building you were held captive in by the Thames, do you remember anything about it? Could you find it again?"

"I... I remember very little."

"Anything, even the smallest detail may prove significant."

"Only the smell. Like a slaughterhouse," and she held her hand to her mouth, trembling. "Those poor women, you must find them... I... wait. I remember, when I was in the cage, the men had a symbol, a tattoo on their hands. A black butterfly."

Miss Summerfly is escorted back to her lodgings by Constable Walnut and placed under police protection. I have advised her to leave London, to stay with her relatives by the sea until this investigation is complete and those responsible arrested. Professor Hummingbird's wedding will be taking place tomorrow morning and I intend to intercept the nuptials. Detective White will travel to Kent to investigate the kidnapping.

BUTTERFLY
everything is cracking
splintering
being

d

e

s

t

r

o *y*

e

d

Romney Marshes, England, 1865
MR ANGELCAKES & MR HUMMINGBIRD

My name is Wesley Angelcakes and my dearest friend is Gabriel Hummingbird. I have known him since I was ten years old. We grew up together in England on the Romney Marsh, in houses near to each other, across that eerie, ghost ridden landscape. We used to pretend we were explorers and dig into the earth. We found Roman coins and fragments of pottery, a flint blade and the skull of a sheep. We collected beetles, horned ones: black hairy legs, emerald eyes, deep set like jewels. We stored them in jars and then gave them mock funerals down wells.

But after a few years we started to both have a deep fascination for butterflies. It became an addiction. Our fathers gave us butterfly nets for our birthdays and we chased those white marshland moths, the pale blue summer flies and the cabbage-eaters. We chased them as the god of the underworld chased Persephone: unyielding, obsessively.

By the time we were eighteen we both had extensive collections and every variety of butterfly in England sat pinned through the heart in our houses. We arranged a trip abroad to South America to collect varieties of the rarest in the world. It took over a year to plan and here we now are.

We are in Peru, exploring an Aztec temple. We've been in South America for two months now and already have a good collection of ghost moths, emperors and dancing flames. The latter is a vibrant pink and orange butterfly. Gabriel has found seven of those, each one he kisses when he captures them.

This particular temple is cool and dark with great vines creeping round our feet and snails the size of teapots softly moving about. We have come here because we have been told that the rarest butterfly in the world has been spotted here. Her name is Angel-Eater and she is also the largest butterfly in the world. We must have her for our collection, for our exhibition in London on our return.

We creep lower into the bowels of the temple, rubble and dark earth piled round our feet, the walls decaying and crumbling. Gabriel holds the torch, which flickers and spits, revealing paintings on the temple walls. Pictures crudely executed, showing the temple steps covered in piles of bodies, an ocean of bodies and a warrior woman standing at the top. At the bottom of the temple, a river is depicted stuffed full of human hearts.

We come to a great stone door, which with a combined effort we manage to heave open.

Inside is a small chamber with an altar, and a picture drawn on the wall of a deity wearing human skin. Gabriel points his finger to the ceiling and we both gasp for there we see an angel-eater, two foot long, wings as black as hell, floating above our heads.

So softly my net sweeps her in, as though a lover plucking a sweetheart onto the dance floor. And in a moment she's dead.

We are both laughing and dancing. As happy as drunk bugs. Gabriel asks me to check the rest of the chamber to see if there are any more beauties hiding. I peek round the corners of the small chamber, move further in. And then I hear the door shut behind me. Gabriel has locked me in and taken the rarest butterfly in the world.

Why am I not surprised?

I don't know how many days it has been but I am
dying. The picture on the wall keeps talking to me.
It wants to wear my skin. I try and fill my mind with
my girls:

Pearl-queen
Cabbage-eater
Ghost
Blue emperor
Dancing flames
Jester-bells
Toad-eye
Devil's finger
Meadowsweet
Maiden-kiss
Butter-shark
Little boy blue

They flicker off my tongue like spit.
Angel-Eater. The biggest.

I tell the picture on the wall my name. I tell him
before I forget it. He likes my name. He likes my
skin. I am forgetting the names of the butterflies. I
start to hallucinate. I have turned into a butterfly
and glide about my tomb. I am a jester-bell, brown

as a leaf in autumn with little red splodges on my wings. I am a little butterfly, quick moving and delicate as a wisp of smoke. See how high I can fly! And then drop, deep and low and skim the prison floor, my tiny wings brushing it like a flower petal across a cheek. For a moment I am so happy. So deliriously happy.

Before I die he crawls into me. Starts to peel off my wings.

The wedding

My wedding dress is as black as the stomach of a demon. A red sash is around my waist. A top hat on my head, the colour of liquorice. Butterfly butterfly butterfly: my wings are my curved silver blades concealed within my high-laced boots. Shall I spread my wings for you?

Mr Angelcakes thinks I look interesting. I say, shouldn't a bride look beautiful? He says I am not an ordinary bride.

Mr Loveheart is throwing stones at my window. I open it and peer down at him. Today he's dressed in white, red hearts like love bites.

"Don't marry him, Boo Boo! He's incredibly dull."

Mr Angelcakes nods his head in agreement, his skin wobbling slightly.

"Are you still going to blow him up?" I say, curiously.

"I'm not spoiling the surprise," he replies. "But I have been considering beating him to death with his own foot."

"I like that," Mr Angelcakes says, **"it's subtle,"** and a piece of his face falls off onto the floor.

"He's too old for you!" says Loveheart, impaling a wind-fallen apple on the point of his sword and examining it.

"He's a magician, and he will turn you into a butterfly again."

"I shall have to decapitate him then, my darling," and bows very low.

"I do hope so, Mr Loveheart," and I shut the window.

The carriage arrives for me in the courtyard. Two black horses, as the Professor had specified, with red feathers in their manes. Mr Angelcakes keeps me company. He is looking forward to today. Grinning to himself, the skin round his lips drooping like melted wax.

"You look good enough to eat," he says fiendishly.

The carriage moves shakily along the woodland path, juddering softly like jelly on a plate. A small note for me rests on the seat:

My Darling Boo Boo,

My prize possession, my Angel-Eater, is staying with a friend in London. She is in safe hands. I felt it best to move her since Detective Waxford's campaign to destroy my reputation. You will serve as a sufficient amusement for me until I am reunited with her.

Your devoted,
Gabriel

"Oh dear, Mr Angelcakes, you won't be getting your butterfly just yet."

The carriage pulls up to the church, which is decorated with heaps of flame-red roses, even on the tombstones. A massacre of flowers. Outside the church, Ignatius Hummingbird awaits me. He will be escorting me down the aisle.

The doors to the church open, revealing row upon row of more blood flowers. The vicar, Mr Wormhole, stands with the Professor near the altar. I can see my brother, Pedrock, sitting with Mrs Charm and Mr Loveheart. Behind them, Grandpa, Aunt Grubweed with Prunella, Estelle and Cornelius, and Reverend Plum smiling nervously. Next to the door is Detective Waxford and standing in the very corner of the church, a man I have never seen before, with an eye-patch and black top hat.

"Who is that man?" I ask Ignatius as we walk down the aisle.

"Mr Cobweb. He is a friend of ours."

Detective Waxford with a face like a grumpy gargoyle approaches us. "Mr Ignatius Hummingbird. I am arresting you for abduction and attempted murder."

"Oh, Detective Waxford, you're making a very stupid mistake."

Waxford takes out his handcuffs, "Either you come willingly or I shoot you," and he withdraws his gun and aims it at Ignatius's head.

"You wouldn't dare."

Waxford pulls the trigger. Pieces of brain splatter my face. Ignatius falls to the floor in a heap. Prunella screams. Mr Loveheart stands up and wanders casually next to the detective, his sword in one hand.

The walls of the church start to compress. Pillars wobble. The Professor, bright red in the face, as though he is about to burst screams; "You can't kill my brother, NO NO NO," and stomps his feet, "You can't have my butterfly, NO NO NO."

Mr Cobweb shuts the church doors and stands by them like a guard dog from hell, removing a long thin blade.

"This is becoming quite interesting," says Mr Loveheart.

The guests are starting to run for the door: the vicar, Mr Wormhole, nimblest on his feet, manages to squeeze himself out of the side window. Cornelius runs to the door and is hacked down by Mr Cobweb, limbs flying over Waxford's head. Waxford shoots Mr Cobweb in the stomach, but Cobweb remains unhurt and stabs Reverend Plum in the throat.

"What?" cries Waxford staring at his gun.

Mr Loveheart throws his sword at Professor Hummingbird, pinning him to the back wall like one of his specimens. I pull the butterfly blades from my boots and approach my fiancé.

Mr Cobweb has Prunella by the leg. He hacks it off and then starts chopping up Estelle. Mrs Charm, following the Vicar, is pushing Pedrock through the side window.

I approach my fiancé.

Bang! Bang! Bang!

Waxford's gun goes off again, no doubt still shooting at Mr Cobweb. A foot flies past Waxford's head and bounces off the pulpit. Waxford is shouting, "This bloody village! I'm retiring after this case!"

The Professor is trying to pull the sword out of his heart.

"My darling butterfly."

"Where is the Angel-Eater?" I say, my blade resting against his throat.

"Somewhere you will not find it, sweetheart," and he starts to laugh. I see Mrs Charm's legs going through the window to her safety.

Bang!

Mr Loveheart shoots Mr Cobweb in the brain.

Mr Cobweb grabs Grandpa and cuts his head off. Aunt Grubweed stands up, picking up a small angel statue, and hits Mr Cobweb over the head with it. He staggers about and then slices the top of her head off with his blade. He jumps out of the window, Waxford shooting at him.

I look again at the Professor. "Last chance."

Mr Angelcakes is clapping and laughing, **"Such fun, such fun!"**

The Professor, "I'm not telling you, you little bitch."

"But YOU must tell her," Mr Angelcakes panics. **"YOU must."**

"NO," he says, and he whispers a word of magic.

Zap!

Everyone else turns into butterflies.

A heap of rainbow wings fluttering about. Some dead on the floor. I can see Mr Loveheart; he's a cherry-glitter red one soaring above the others. I am transfixed by this magic; I smile, half bewitched.

Professor Hummingbird pulls the sword out of his stomach and grabs me by the hair. The butterflies soar and whizz round us, swoop in circles, move in spirals.

He presses his hands round my head, squeezes my skull.

I am on my knees; I am pulled under the weights of his magic. I shut my eyes; I shut my eyes and I see hovering in black space: the Angel-Eater. Huge, opening its wings. A book turning pages.

My name is written on its wings.

The Professor kills me with a kiss. Venom. Murderer of butterflies. It seeps through my skin: black in my veins. My story is ending.

And I see, I see the red butterfly of Mr Loveheart dazzle and float on air: the shape of a heart.

I raise my blades, slice the Professor in half.

His scream is the sound of glass breaking. The butterflies in his house are flying out of their confines, a whirlwind of wings beating at a hundred miles an hour. The butterflies in the church turn back into people. Hit the floor with a *thud*.

But the favourite, the Angel-Eater, is still behind glass, and Mr Angelcakes is weeping.

Death has arrived.

"Hello, Boo Boo," he says, in a voice like liquid silver. Eyes like black mirrors and he holds out a hand and helps me off the floor. "You'd better come with me."

"No."

"Excuse me?"

"I said 'no'."

He grabs me by the arm and starts dragging me along the floor, but Mr Loveheart intervenes suddenly and sweeps me up in his arms and kisses me.

Time has no meaning anymore. It is electricity! We are sparks!

"What do you think you are doing, Loveheart?" demands a very annoyed Death.

"I am saving her, for I am the Lord of the Underworld and my kiss will bring the dead back to life." He takes a bag of rhubarb and custard sweeties out of his pocket and offers me one.

"Unbelievable! I will require some *compensation* for this blatant disregard for the natural laws."

"Of course," smiles Loveheart and offers him a boiled sweet.

Detective Waxford is banging on the entrance of the church.

"Someone open the fucking door!" he shouts.

Mrs Charm opens obliges, "Ah! You're still alive, detective."

"There's a pile of dead people in here!" he cries.

"Surely it's not that bad," she replies, and we all turn to view the heap of body parts splattered over the church floor. Waxford walks outside, tripping up over the dead body of Reverend Plum on the way out and cursing loudly.

Mr Loveheart takes my hand. "I believe you are now available for courtship."

Loveheart and Boo Boo

I have taken Boo Boo home with me to my Palace of Hearts. My little insect queen. All my hearts are yours.

She plays with the heads in my trees, those dangling trinkets. She licks the heart-shaped lollypops.

We drink hot chocolate, dance round my gardens. I chase her like a butterfly with a net. Jump through hoops for her. This is what love is: it makes all the clocks go backwards, brings the dead back to life. Grave-leaping. Time breaking.

The roses in my gardens are love bombs: they are exploding.

Waiting for butterflies

I sleep in the big bed of hearts, beside Mr Loveheart. I dream of the Angel-Eater opening her wings like a prayer book.

WINGS ARE PAGES. PAGES ARE WINGS. READ ME.

WORSHIP ME.

She speaks. "You will find me. You will find me behind glass."

I spread butterfly wings on my toast.

Open a pot of marmalade.

Talk to my knife.

I wonder whether I am made of question marks?

??????????
?   ?   ?

PART THREE

The Houses of Parliament
ZADOCK HEAP EATING A BATTENBERG

I've been thinking about that little prince, Mr Loveheart, all day; he keeps popping into my head for some unfathomable reason. Mmmmm. I take a piece of the Battenberg and crush it between my teeth. Succulent squeeze.

Hanging on my office wall, above my head is the Angel-Eater, a butterfly as black as a hole in space, as red as a heart. She's beating her wings, trying to get out. Like my women in cages. They refuse to accept their confinement; they refuse to accept they are my food.

YOU ARE A CAKE, MY DARLING. SHOW ME YOUR CREAM.

I like to construct boundaries; I like to form edges on spaces. KEEP YOU WITHIN THE LINES.

My mind is unsettled at the moment; I keep

twiddling my thumbs.

A knock at the door.

"Come in," I say, yawning.

Mr Evening-Star enters, his voice a quiver, "Good afternoon, Prime Minister. I have come to inform you that all of the arrangements are ready for this evening."

"Excellent," I sigh.

"I also have some rather bad news, I'm afraid. Both Ignatius and Gabriel Hummingbird are dead."

"Really?" Something interesting at last.

"Yes, a most unfortunate occurrence. Slaughtered at a wedding."

"And who killed them?" I lean forward and a suspicion creeps into my thoughts. A symbol, a heart on as string, floats in my head.

"Well," he replies nervously, "It appears Ignatius was shot in the head by a Detective Waxford of Scotland Yard for refusing to be arrested."

"I like the sound of this plucky Detective Waxford."

"And Gabriel was sliced in half by his sixteen year-old bride-to-be. A girl named Boo Boo."

I glance up at the Angel-Eater in the frame. "Ahhh, the little butterfly girl. I would very much like to… meet her."

"And another gentleman was also involved: a Mr Loveheart. Mr Cobweb informs me that this Mr Loveheart can bring the dead back to life with a kiss, which is quite an unusual gift. Considering the astronomical murder statistics in London, power over death would be a formidable asset. Why only this morning I witnessed a man hit over the head with a privy door!"

My heart stops.

"WHAT... What did you say?" I gasp.

"Privy door. Apparently, according to an infamous and deranged linguist, of all the phrases in the English language, 'Privy door' is the most beautiful."

I held him up in the air by the throat.

"Ah." He squeezed the words out. "I see that is perhaps not the information you required!"

"I'm waiting, Mr Evening-Star!"

"Mr Loveheart can kiss the dead and bring them back to life."

I am shaking. "This is not possible," and I drop him on the floor and grip the sides of the desk compressing it until it shatters.

"Sir? Do you know him?"

"I have had the curious pleasure of meeting him," I spit out the words of boiled rage.

"Um, do you require anything from me, Prime

Minister? A cup of tea or perhaps a nice, buttery egg?" He creeps towards the door.

"GET OUT BEFORE I WHIP THE SKIN OFF YOU!"

"Of course, Prime Minister," a glassy smile on his lips; he delicately shuts the door, slipping out of existence.

The Angel-Eater is beating its wings in the frame behind me, pin through its heart, trying to break free.

I crush the Battenberg under my fist. Pound it into the remains of the desk.

LOVEHEART
BASH!
LOVEHEART
BOOM!
LOVEHEART
SPLAT!

Zedock Heap visits the British Museum

After murdering the Battenberg I slip out into the streets of London; head towards the museum. I need a little fresh air; it will calm the bubbling under my skin, sooooothe the pressure. I think about pulling Mr Loveheart's head off and sucking on his spinal cord. Little prince, little prince, you DARE step into my fairy tale, you DARE try to rearrange my story. I am the OGRE. The MAN-EATER. SURVIVAL OF THE FITTEST, MR LOVEHEART, AND I AM THE BIGGEST.

I think about my women in cages, screaming, begging for their lives. MEAT. MEAT MEAT. That is all you are in my world. I think about the bottle of cherry wine I will sup tonight when I eat one of them. Savour the vintage; uncork and let it BREATHE.

I AM YOUR PRIME MINISTER AND YOU NEED TO FEED ME ENGLAND.

My mood is black.

I change the colour of the Thames to mirror my thoughts. I can shift London into whatever shape I choose. Ripple and sludge. Simmer and boil. I move across London, past the filth, past the flesh, past the stink of you all. My footsteps mark the city. I leave my imprint. Hell is, after all, only a few inches below. Can you feel the red? Can you feel the heat under your feet?

I walk into the bright box of space. I change the colour of the sky; a flash of green lightning strikes St Paul's. Unexpected ! I move onwards. My mood as black as dungeons. Loveheart on my mind. LOVEHEART ALWAYS ON MY MIND.

The creatures of London are wobbly lines, something drawn from a sketchbook with charcoal. They can be smudged out. Top-hated rich gentlemen are deformed bird-men on the paper. Bright-eyed, pretty ladies in their rainbow dresses become screaming tropical birds, fanning themselves and twittering nervously. Black swirls of charcoal, nothing more.

And those lower, darker forms of London, the creatures of the underworld: the feeble, the half dead with their wretchedness, starvation and filth, the cheap scent of lavender on the gutter-piss girls, their black toothless mouths, the enormous emptiness.

A canvas. That is all you are London. A canvas for my artistry. HAND ME A PAINTBRUSH. Let me give you a lesson in creation.

You open your mouth like a money-box. You'll swallow what I give you.

The whores round the horse trough, washing their thighs, tongue waggling lies. Exhausted, worn down, swamped in sadness, they cluster together: a mass of bruised flesh, putrid insides, black lungs and rotting bones. The vast sky above them swirls and simmers, savage green – the soupy concoction of a sorcerer. I click my fingers. MAKE THEM MOVE.

Horse shit stuck between their swollen toes. They stick fingers in their mouths, count their remaining teeth. A backside pinched by a grubby face drunk. They are the foul little specimens. I glide past. I AM THE SHARK.

I AM THE SHARK.

I am being observed by a man with porridge stains on his waistcoat. I have seen him before. He comes out in the darkness. Yellow fingernails, leech fat fingers. Killer of women; girls go missing all the time; slip off the edges of the world. Fall into holes.

I stare into him, make him evaporate. MELT ON THE SPOT.

I leave him behind, move past the butchers, where bloody sausages hang in sloppy ribbons from a hook in the window. The butcher examines me as I pass: one big hairy hand clutching a glittering wet intestinal loop.

Meandering through the maze of side alleys, I make my way towards the museum. The sludge-brown streets are bobbing with excrement, bubbling foul odours: the stench of tanneries, pie shops and soap-boilers. I gaze into the cobwebbed window of a Hocus-pocus den: see a human skull painted blue, and tiny fairy-size candles sizzling in the darkness. Inside, hovering over a dirty crystal ball, a decrepit looking gent peers goggle-eyed into the future. He wears a tattered robe of indigo with embroidered stars, now falling off. What future does he see? What other-worlds can he glimpse?

I AM FROM THE OTHERWORLDS, FORTUNE TELLER.

I AM FROM THE UNDERNEATH.

ONLY AN INCH AWAY.

• • •

I stride through the narrow streets, passing rows of shops: smell pickles, dead dog, green cheeses and hot cider. I could gobble up the lot.

I am blistering black, blacker than midnight, blacker than space.

I AM THE SHARK.

The museum gates loom open, the jaws of a beast carved in marble. The sky is full of spirals of milky clouds, whipped up white. I turn them green. Sour the palette.

I am an executioner today, I imagine a thousand skulls lie under my feet.

POWER.

Loops of energy spin round me, demonic atoms colliding and exploding. Do you want to know what power is?

I pick out a small gentleman in the crowd carrying a heavy pile of books. He staggers under their weight, wobbles on his feet. I have chosen him.

He explodes; pieces of his body splatter a school party. A small child holds up a severed arm with delight. His teacher, drenched in intestinal juices, screams, "PUT THAT DOWN THIS INSTANT, PERCY!"

Percy looks disappointed. That's education for you.

I tip my hat at him.

Percy waves back, then turns his attention away, looking for the head.

I am in a world of skulls. The pieces of you.

I take off my coat. Reveal my waistcoat, which is quite extraordinary: embroidered with exquisite lizards and butterflies in a dazzle of aqua and cornflower blues. I am getting hot. I feel the boil in my blood.

Young women drift past: they smell of buttercups, bluebells and raspberry jelly. Not really my thing at all. I like my women to taste like fireworks. Melt in my hands. Under my weight.

And here comes the spindly curator Uriah Cushing, hunched very low, his words a muttering wetness. "Prime Minister, it is an honour to see you again."

I nod, acknowledge his feeble existence.

"And may I say," he blithers on, "your last donation to the museum was considerable."

He's a nervous little creature, hook nosed, fearful of predators. Smells of something *cabbagy*. Everything has to be labelled and positioned carefully within white spaces in his world. The wondrous and magical are stuffed into glass jars and corked, sealed within a vacuum. Never to be released.

I follow him up the great stone steps into the mouth of the museum: my eyes wandering to the heights of the vast ceiling where, hanging from wires within the gloomy depths, the complete skeleton of a great dinosaur is ominously suspended above us. I listen for the creak of chains. I listen for the breaking.

We move into dark indigo space.

"I have an interest in viewing the bottled mermaids," I say to Uriah, who leads me up the flight of steps to the upper level of the museum.

Within a glass cabinet sits a monstrous stuffed frog, observing quietly.

Within the velvety black shadows of a corner of the exhibition, a pickled giant octopus floats in a jar of formaldehyde, a weird creature of surveillance.

I imagine the curator stuffed and preserved within a cabinet. The thought amuses me.

Uriah points to the cabinet, "Here are the beauties."

BEAUTY BEAUTY
I HAVE SEEN SUPERNOVAS.
YOUR BEAUTY IS A PIECE OF SHRIVELLED SKIN IN A JAR.

I peer at the bottled mermaids. There are a dozen of them, misshapen and pickled. Soft green and purple-veined. They have eyes like huge white spaces, as though buried under deep snow. I want to pluck out their eyeballs. Taste them.

In my mind, I move charcoal over the paper, catch them, the little fish women. Catch them on powdery sheets, fingers black with dust.

Now I want to look at the dinosaur. I like its bones. All crack and splinter. I want to feel its great teeth. I look over the balcony. I see two little girls. Sweet as a custard tart. I want to eat them up. They are part of a guided tour squeezing down the narrow corridors, wafting a stench of mutton fat and tobacco. I can see the mummified Pygmy midgets, with scissor-smiles. Snap Snap Snap. Teeth biting bone. Teeth biting bone.

And then I smell him.

LOVEHEART!

I peer over the balcony; he's within the guided tour. He's wearing green with red hearts exploding all over his coat. And he's with the butterfly girl. She's like a bottled mermaid; she's been pickled in a weird formula. I want to stick my fingers in her jar. She's carrying weaponry! Unbelievable! You'd think there would be some sort of security.

The tour guide, who is a hunched dwarf, screams, "And so he died from a festering wound!" and then "If we can hurry along, there are some fascinating examples of cannibalism in the next room."

Loveheart looks up and I speak over the tour guide: "And if our paths cross ever again, Mr Loveheart, AND IF OUR PATHS EVER CROSS AGAIN."

I begin to descend the great staircase. The bottled mermaids explode in their jars.

The butterfly girl throws a blade at me. It *zizzes*... impales my top hat to the wall. I am impressed! I am laughing.

Loveheart, Boo Boo and bottled mermaids

"What a coincidence!" I shout out, "We JUST keep running into one another," and I draw my sword.

"YOU ARE A PIECE OF SHIT ON MY BOOT THAT NEEDS REMOVING!" he bellows.

Boo Boo launches herself up the stairs and leaps into the air, blade aimed at his head.

Heap grabs her by the throat and pulls her to the ground.

As quick as a wink she spins her blade and sinks it into his heart.

He staggers backwards. Pulls the blade out, "You have completely ruined my waistcoat !" and holds her by the hair, in midair.

"LET HER GO!" I demand.

"Or what?" he laughs.

He clicks his fingers. She disappears. Reappears

behind him inside a glass cabinet of the mermaids. Suspended in water. Bashing her fists against magic glass

"*Boo Boo!*" I shout and leap up the stairs. Hack into him.

The curator appears, "Gentleman! Could I ask you to desist?"

The demon pulls the curator's head off with his hands; it rolls down the steps, tomato-red splattering the glass coffin, within which a stuffed crocodile smirks.

The guided tour screams and segments. The tour guide glances at his clipboard in bewilderment, the head bounces playfully down the steps and rolls by his feet.

I smash the glass, the water falls out and Boo Boo tumbles into my arms. She coughs water, grits her teeth.

I AM LORD OF THE UNDERWORLD.

Energies loop and sizzle.

I AM OUTSIDE YOUR RULES.

I stab my sword into the demon's gut. He grabs me, pulls me closer to his face. "I am having you for dinner."

We disappear in an explosion of sparks.

The house of Zedock Heap

I awake on an immense bloody-red velvet-cushioned bed. I YAWN!

The room smells of Turkish delight. I am a sugar cube! I AM A SUGAR CUBE!

I wonder if I have I been drugged?

I was dreaming, I remember. I was dreaming I was a Lord of the Underworld. My name was written upside down on paper stars. Each one a part of me. Each one dangling on golden thread; wobbling in deep space.

Perhaps I have been dissected. *Oooops!* I fall off the bed.

My legs buckle under me. Where is my sword?

I hold the bed post, prop myself up. My name is Heart.

My name is HEART. I have a cat. He is very fat.

He is a fat cat. I love my fat cat.

I'm in a bedroom! So much red, it hurts my eyes. The walls are made up of roots which intertwine with one another and they are moving. The walls are alive! I touch them and they swell and then spiral in my hand. I examine the doorway – a red portal with a black wet hole for a lock.

This is a very odd place and my brain feels rather soft. Perhaps I should have a little sleep, dream of icing sugar, dream of spaces made of sugar.

A great watery mirror hangs on the wall above the bed and it shimmers. I can see sea-worms and small opaque starburst-fish swim within its depths. I stick my hand into the mirror and remove it, dripping and glistening. The looping roots begin to entwine around me and pull me across the floor to the vast bed which splits open like a flower. It has fangs!

On a small table by the bed sits a solitary book. I reach for it, my fingers fondling the cover which is made with human skin! How very curious! This book must belong to a mad man!

The Vinegar Doctor

There is no author. I open at a random page:

"It excites you, doesn't it?"

This is indeed a very ODD thing. What was the last thing I recall? Mmmmmm, I think I was talking to a butterfly. I was kissing a butterfly. I saw a shark, I saw a shark. I SAW A SHARK.

I pick another page:

> **Black as boiling nightfall. Unripe fruits hung like poisonous gifts, lustrous greens, other-worldly blues, beetle blacks, devil reds, pomegranate.**

Whose bedroom is this? Some sort of demon I can only presume. My mind is a little muddled, a spoon in the jam.

blOOd-orange
blOOd-orange
blOOd-orange   blOOd-orange
blOOd-orange   blOOd-orange   blOOd-orange blOOd-orange

Brain damage perhaps? Am I inside a fairytale? IF SO, who am I? I am the black-eyed prince. I am the thing that kills the wicked magician. I AM THE LORD OF THE DEAD. I reanimate you!

Come here and give me a kiss.

I recall I ate rice pudding with a splodge of marmalade for dinner.

Inside the forest there are dead shiny creatures.

I wonder if anyone will bring me supper for I am awfully hungry. Perhaps some toast? Thickly buttered.

I eat eerie bulging-eyed insects.

Am I within a dream. Inside a space, a room, a brain? Tiny flowers of starlight. I REMEMBER! My name is JOHN and I like cake.

Don't be alarmed. Everyone is made of marzipan.

How curious. I pick another page

You will have to eat your way out, Mr Loveheart.
Or cut his head off.

Aha! A book that is helping me. Now, where is my sword?

You're standing on it.

Ah! Yes of course. Thank you.

You're welcome.

I shut the book. I think I am a PRINCE. I am a fairytale. I am a fairytale. I look in the mirror at my face. I have black eyes. That, perhaps, isn't quite normal.

I move closer to the surface of ripple, up to the curious mirror. Am I a demon prince? I feel my heart beat. I feel the thud, the spongy *thud thud thud*. I remember now. Ah, I understand, I am a bit broken inside. *THUD THUD THUD.*

I am quite mad.

THUD THUD THUD.

I am not really human anymore. I want to step inside the mirror, wiggle my toes under the waters. BECOME LIQUID.

A creak!

The door opens and a queer-looking butler, for he is wearing a pink turban and holding a blowpipe, enters.

"Mr Loveheart, you are required for dinner," and he shoots the pipe. A dart hits me in the thigh.

"I feel rather ill-used!" I proclaim before it oozes into my bloodstream. Fizzing, wobbly jelly, wobbly jelly wobbly jelly.

I hear a screech, see him bring in an old iron wheelchair which he plops me into, squeaks me off down the corridor. Into a darkness that oozes. Rather splendid plum velvet walls dripping with splodges of vanilla scented wax. Lots of tapestries hanging about the place, withery dithery!

"I don't believe I have any tapestries at Loveheart Manor," I say to the butler. "Or, come to think on it, there may be just one, of an infamous and weird-bearded ancestor – in the basement."

The butler ignores me.

"I am feeling rather wooooooooozy."

I see the pretty pictures: a knight is battling a great white coiled worm. Poppy red, bone white, sea serpent green, Aztec gold. They fizzle and dazzle my head. Eggy splat and green jelly flubber. Oohh another one. A mermaid the colour of seaweed splat and foam. She wriggles, she giggles, fish tail question mark.

I sink out of the chair, stare at the carpet, "IT IS BLUE!" I shriek.

Tapestry tapestry: black dragon, a maiden tied to a tree, waiting to be devoured. She is smiling. How extraordinary!

Fairytale fairytale fairytale fairytale SPRUNG to life leap from the walls!

I AM WITHIN A FAIRYTALE.

The wheel chair squeaks, "AND THE CARPET IS BLUE!"

TAPESTRY tapestry tapestry: this time a magician in a top hat speckled with stars, sawing in half a girl confined within a magic box.

"MAGIC BOX!" I shout, "MAGIC BOX." Above him hangs a moon, a wax egg. "I WOULD LIKE SOME CUSTARD."

The butler sighs wearily and opens a door into a dining room, a room with food on a big red dining room table. I see custard tarts, macaroons, butterfly cakes, sponge fingers, gingerbread! I want to gobble up the goodies, suck my fingers of sugar.

There is a man at the head of the table. A big man. I KNOW HIM! HE IS THE SHARK.

"Hello, Mr Shark!" and I wave.

He looks happy and his words are all jelly squish and cherry flavoured. I don't understand, but I watch his lips move. Gums like a rubbery fish. He has got a big spoon in his hands.

I am wheeled to the table. In front of me is a big trifle dish.

The butler pours me wine. He smells of peppermint and formaldehyde – corpse preservation stink.

"Why is my head funny?" I say.

His lips move and his words move in a jumble. "Demonic paralysis. Feebles the brain, Mr Loveheart. It affects anything of our kind."

"I have a feeble brain!" I announce, followed by, "May I have a bowl of trifle please?" I point to the wall behind him. I see a big butterfly in a frame. It is moving. "It is alive!" I shout.

"Yes, of course," he smiles – oh so many teeth – and steps closer to me. He eliminates the space. I know what the butterfly is; it zaps into my brain.

"BOO BOO," I shout, "BOO BOO NEEDS THAT BUTTERFLY."

"She is a predator," he speaks. "Isn't she beautiful?" He taps the glass. "She is the only one in the world. It's funny how you don't appreciate something until it is gone. Until it is no more. Will someone miss you, Mr Loveheart, when you are eaten?"

"I believe my cat would miss me." My head rolls backwards. On the ceiling is deep space. I see planets dangle, a shooting star whizzzzes past. Comets collide. Black sparkle and a whiff of sulphur.

"You have a very unusual ceiling!" I remark.

He put his hand on my shoulder. "You and I cannot coexist, Mr Loveheart. That is the way of things, the way of survival of the species. You are the competition and you concern me and yet, you are insane. Your brain is a cauliflower. Why should you worry me? Mad little prince! Hell has dominion over this world. My queen, the Queen of Hell, is conquering the planet, her armies, her navies, claiming new territories. And she sits on the throne of England and rules already a quarter of the earth. We are eating you up little world. We are gobbling you up. Humans! You are a food source for us. That is all you are."

"I have to stop you," and my head is fizzzzzzing and I try to lift my sword but I can't.

"Stop me? You are a fool. Your head is full of sponge," and he laughs, rich treacle laughter. It soaks into the wallpaper, slips over me. He puts his mouth close to my ear, whispers, "I have eaten stardust. It tastes like sugar."

We are inside a book of fairy tales and the pages are turning themselves. My head feels so heavy, my heart is the *THUD THUD THUD*.

"Red is the colour of my heart" I laugh "RED RED RED RED," and my head sags and plops into the trifle dish.

Oh dear.

I am the melting blue of space. I AM AN ASTEROID.

CATCH ME!

Rufus Hazard to the rescue!

I have just left Miss Pussywillow's House of Delight. What a splendid evening that was. I was whipped within an inch of my life by a spirited mistress of the cat o'nine tails called Big Gertrude. A most pleasant evening it was and an excellent roast peasant supper at my club beforehand with a marvellous plum pudding and custard. What more can a man ask for than a good flogging and a decent pudding?

Well buggeration! That odd fellow, Mr Death, has materialised in front of me.

"Mr Hazard, I require your assistance. Mr Loveheart is in peril."

"Egad! Peril is my middle name! What can I do to help the young whelp?"

"Really?"

"Of course, Rufus Peril Hazard at your service."

"Do you have your machete with you?"

I smile, show my teeth and whip my old trusty machete from its sheath on my back. It glimmers under moonlight.

TWING!

"Excellent, the prime minister is about to eat him. Number 7, Flumpet Court. I need to find Boo Boo. Can you manage?"

"Flumpet Court, I know the place. Never fear, Mr Death, I'll sort that cad Heap out and rescue Loveheart!"

I arrive under a bold moon and knock briskly on the rather smart red door. A suspicious looking butler wearing a pink turban and holding a blow pipe opens the door.

"I am Rufus Hazard and I believe your employer has FOUL intentions towards a very dear friend of mine, a Mr Loveheart. I understand he is being held against his will and … WHAT THE HELL ARE YOU DOING WITH A BLOW PIPE?"

He shuts the door in my face. The *cad!*

I shout, "DOORS DO NOT STOP RUFUS HAZARD!" before I boot it with my foot. The door flies off its hinges and collapses. I step over the remains of door and glare at the whimpering butler who tries to blow pipe me! The dart hits the wall and I swipe my machete, slicing the legs off the snivelling coward. His torso glides past me, and out the door screaming.

"THAT IS FOR TRYING TO BLOW PIPE ME, YOU IMPERTINENT SCOUNDREL!"

I storm the corridor and boot in the dining room door, appreciating the excellent tapestries and stuffed badger on the mantelpiece. It is difficult to acquire experts in taxidermy in London.

Mr Loveheart is lying face down, head in a trifle dish. The prime minister looms over him with a curious shaped spoon.

"STEP AWAY FROM HIM OR YOU'LL FEEL MY BLADE, HEAP!" and I stick my leg up on the chair and swipe the blade; it glints under candle light.

The prime minister looks genuinely surprised. "Who the hell are you?"

"Rufus Hazard. Earl of Derbyshire, and *that*, I believe is a brain spoon." I point my weaponry at the accursed object.

He puts the spoon down on the table and sighs. "I am going to skin you alive and then suck your eyeballs out of your head."

"TRY IT, SHIT-HEAP. I DARE YOU!" I scream.

The walls of the house squeeze, the ceiling wobbles.

A dart hits the prime minister in the forehead.

Boo Boo is behind me.

"BITCH!" he cries, and slumps to the ground.

Mr Loveheart stirs and lifts his head, which is covered in custard, and smiles at me. "Rufus! Hello. I think I am a pudding!"

"Dear old sock, take my arm," and I help him up.

Boo Boo points at the framed picture of a giant butterfly on the wall, "Rufus, get it for me!"

I step closer but the room is filling with blood. Knee high, I wade through towards the butterfly but there is too much blood and it is rising!

"Boo Boo, we have to get out quickly." Too late! We are washed away on a wave along the corridors, fast out the door into the street.

A voice, that villain Zedock, soars over the blood and he's laughing. *Ha ha ha ha ha ha ha ha ha ha ha ha ha ha ha ha.*

What black magic is this? And before I can step back inside to chop the villain's head off, the house vanishes in a tidal wave of blood. HITS US. SLAPS US ABOUT. Carries us down the streets of London. FASTER, FASTER, FASTER. I try to grab a lamp post and fail, scream and get dragged as fast as a bullet across London. Ooze and foul slop of red. It goes down my mouth, into my eyes and nose. I see Boo

Boo whizzz past – and is that Loveheart floating in a star shape in the distance?

We are vomited out into Hyde Park in a violent explosion of red.

I awake face down, disorientated by a park bench. Boo Boo is shaking Mr Loveheart, who is still somewhat delirious and talking about jam.

I stand up and raise my machete. "This is not over, Zedock Heap."

Detective Sergeant White and Constable Walnut meet Mr Poppy

Walnut and I are in Spitalfields outside the Magic Emporium, and we're wondering if Mr Ink-Squid may have some information on the butterfly symbol. Waxford thinks he might come in useful.

"Did I ever tell you that my great grandfather was an amateur magician, sir?" says Walnut, scratching his chin.

"I don't believe so," I sigh.

"Well, he was. Pulled dead rabbits out of his hat. Tried to saw my grandmother in half. His career had an untimely ending when the stage collapsed at Brighton pier and he knocked himself unconscious. He never recovered. Couldn't remember who he was."

"There's always a silver lining in every cloud of misfortune," I reply, opening the door to the Magic Emporium. A large, black-bearded gentleman stands behind the counter.

"Mr Otto Ink-Squid?"

"Yes," he replies.

"My name is Detective Sergeant White and this is Constable Walnut. I believe you have already spoken to Detective Waxford. We were hoping you might be able to help us with our investigation."

Mr Ink-Squid nods. "What do you need?"

"We are investigating the kidnapping of a young woman. She was transported to a gentlemen's club by the river Thames and kept in a cage. The members of this club had a black butterfly symbol on their hands. We need to know what information you have on any unusual groups operating in the London area."

"You mean cults? Do I know of any cults in London?"

"Yes, do you?"

"I have heard of this butterfly cult. But only heard rumours. They are one of the more extreme cults and extremely difficult to join. I know of a man who is involved with them on a lower level. He helps them with transportation."

"You mean kidnapping?"

"Very likely. He's an undertaker. His name is Mr Poppy. His establishment is round the corner;

there's usually a few coffins propped up against the shop wall."

"Do you have any idea what this butterfly cult do with the women?"

"I really don't know. I don't like to think what these people get up to," Ink-Squid says, sadly.

"What have you heard about them?"

"I've heard Mr Poppy gets a lot of money for disposing of the corpses."

We leave the Magic Emporium and in a few hundred yards find Mr Poppy's undertaking establishment. Mr Ink-Squid was right, half a dozen wooden coffins line the entrance, as though pillars into the underworld.

"This is a bit creepy," says Constable Walnut.

"Death is always a bit creepy, Walnut."

We enter the gloomy premises, the black letters of **MR POPPY** above our heads, malign, sinister marks. Inside, a very tall skeletal man, wearing a black undertaker's coat and top hat with a purple feather, sits taking tea and crumpets. He looks over a hundred years old, face withered away, skin stretched over his skull like parchment. The remaining white wisps of his hair hang like loose threads from under his top hat. He looks at us suspiciously whilst devouring the remainder of his crumpet.

"So, who has died?" he says chuckling.

"Possibly your reputation," I reply.

"Who are you?" his smile removed, wiping butter from his lips.

"Detective Sergeant White and Constable Walnut, sir. We'd like to ask you some questions."

"I'm rather busy, gentlemen. Come back tomorrow," and he starts eating another crumpet.

"Who is your employer, Mr Poppy?"

"I am the owner, but I suppose my employer in a broader sense would be Death," and he looks very amused with himself.

"Very funny. What can you tell me about the Butterfly Club?"

Mr Poppy's face stretches into ice. "Never heard of them."

"Really? I was under the belief that you got rid of the dead bodies for them."

"Rumours ain't proof." He sneers and throws a crumpet at Walnut's head, which *boings* off and out the door.

"That's assaulting a police officer," says Walnut, and whips out his handcuffs.

"I ONLY FREW A FUCKING CRUMPET AT YOU, THAT AIN'T ASSAULT!"

"Assault with a deadly weapon," replies Walnut,

approaching him.

"EXPLAIN TO ME HOW A CRUMPET IS DEADLY?" screams Mr Poppy in exasperation.

Walnut picks up the crumpet and punches him in the face with it. Mr Poppy falls off his chair and lies on the floor unmoving.

I turn, quite astonished to Walnut. "Sometimes you really surprise me."

He grins. "Thank you, sir."

Mr Poppy after a while regains consciousness and stands up rather creakily and removes a pistol from his jacket. Points it at my head.

"Boys!" he shouts. Two rather burly looking meat-heads appear. "Boys," repeats Mr Poppy.

"Yes, Dad?" one of them replies.

"We have a little problem."

Walnut and I are escorted at gunpoint into the back room, where two large black coffins rest.

"Get in," Mr Poppy says, waggling the gun in my face.

"Now Mr Poppy…" I say, trying to reason with him.

"Get in!" he screeches.

The coffin lid shuts with a gentle click. Mr Poppy's fingers tap the surface, humming to himself. I can see nothing. I am submerged in inky blackness.

I hear Mr Poppy's toad-croaking voice above me, "Silly policemen. Really, what were you thinking?"

A few hours pass and then I can feel the coffin being lifted and the lid tapped again.

"Detective..." Mr Poppy is laughing. "You're off to be buried. A lovely little spot in St Augustine's churchyard. Ha ha ha ha."

I pound my fists against the lid. "Release me!"

Ooh I had a little sleep. Feel much better now. I am lying on a pink sofa being fed buttered tea cakes and Turkish coffee.

"A man must have his teacake," says Rufus stuffing one into his mouth. "How are you feeling old boy? Have the drugs worn off yet?"

My head is a fuzz.

"I have always had the feeling that the prime minister was an unscrupulous cad!" sniffs Rufus, and passes me a teacake with extra splodge of jam.

I have a fluffy blanket and cushion for my head. Boo Boo is also eating a teacake, and reading Mrs Charm's novel, *The Cannibal Bishop of Edinburgh*, which I have heard is a murder mystery set in a sinister Abbey and involves missing monks and a suspicious gigantic shepherds' pie.

"When you feel better, you must *decapitate* that wretch Heap. Give him a good thrashing. Unspeakable bad manners leaving a man with his head in a bowl of trifle."

Death appears with a basket of fruit. "Feeling better?"

"I have a terrible headache and ghastly flashbacks about spoons," I say and bite into the teacake.

Death hands me a banana. "Get to St Augustine's Church as soon as possible. Detective White and Constable Walnut are experiencing a premature burial."

To the rescue!

St Augustine's Church is tiny, decrepit and overrun with weeds. Apart from the dead body of a vagrant lying face down on the path, the only source of activity is a funeral service where two coffins are being lowered into the earth by two large ruffians. A bedraggled vicar is reading a mumbled sermon. He appears to be drunk. I grab Boo Boo's hand.

"I think we've found them!" We approach the ruffians boldly.

"Hello, gentlemen," I say. "So whom are you burying today?"

The vicar, whose eyes are red and bulging, begins to speak, but belches rather loudly instead, to his own mortification.

"Never heard of them," I reply.

"Open the coffins," Boo Boo says, pointing her

blades at one of the thugs. He laughs, which is often, I have discovered, a mistake with her. One of her blades embeds itself in his brain and he falls aside like a sack of potatoes. The vicar screams like a little girl.

"Open the coffins," she repeats to the other thug, who obediently does as she requests. She then shoots the other of her blades into his brain like an arrow.

"Ooooooh, good shot!" I cry, clapping my hands.

Constable Walnut and Detective White emerge from their tombs, shaken but steady. I keep an eye on the vicar.

"You should be ashamed of yourself."

"I had no idea they were alive," he replies, nervously.

"Oh really?"

Walnut wobbles and grips a headstone for balance.

"Are you alright, Walnut?" asks Boo Boo.

"Not really. I think I'm having a little panic attack."

"Breathe deep, constable!" Detective White slaps him hard across the back. "We're alive!"

"Thank you, sir. I feel like someone's done something funny to my brain." Walnut pokes his skull. "Have they?"

"I ask myself that same question every day," White replies, and then looks to me, "Where's Waxford?"

"He's here in London."

Boo Boo informs them of naughty Zedock Heap's demonic and cannibalistic persuasion and that he now has possession of the Angel-Eater.

"Frankly, nothing surprises me anymore," sighs Detective White.

"Who would have expected that!" said Walnut, "That our very own prime minister eats people. Well, it's not normal, is it?"

"Sometimes it amazes me that you've never been promoted. How many years have you been a constable, Walnut?" says Detective White.

"Well, if you include the ten years I spent hanging on a wall, metamorphosed into an insect by a perverted sorcerer, about thirty-two years, sir."

"Walnut, return to Detective Waxford and inform him of what has happened and arrest that dodgy vicar. Boo Boo, Loveheart, you will both come with me."

"Where are we going?" asks Boo Boo

"To extract some information from an under-taker," he replies.

We have Mr Poppy tied to a chair in his basement and I punch him in the face and it feels wonderful. He screams, his skull vibrating. Loveheart and Boo Boo stand either side of him, holding an arm each.

"Let's start again, shall we? What do you know about the Butterfly Club?"

"Sod off," Mr Poppy says.

"Oh, that's charming. Such bad manners," tuts Mr Loveheart.

I punch him again, a good hard slog. "I'm waiting, Mr Poppy."

He starts to laugh rather manically.

Boo Boo impales one of her blades in his thigh. His scream is ear-drum shattering.

"This is the last time I am going to ask you, and

273

then I'm going to let her chop you up...
understand?"

"I only collect," he says, fearfully.

"Collect what?"

"The women. I collect them."

"Where is the Butterfly Club?"

"I don't know. Please, I just pick up the bodies."

"From where?"

"By the river. There's an old theatre, the Dancing
Imp. They dump the bodies on the stage."

"When are you collecting them next?"

"Tomorrow. Midnight."

"From whom do you collect the bodies?"

"Mr Cobweb."

Mr Loveheart is sitting on the desk, flicking idly
through his diary. "Ooh look, on Tuesday he
purchased a shovel!"

Ignoring Mr Loveheart, I continue, "Is Zedock
Heap the leader of the Butterfly Club?"

Mr Poppy grits his teeth. "I don't know who's the
boss."

"Who else is involved?"

"I don't know anything else. You'll just have to
kill me."

Boo Boo slices his head off. It bounces against the
wall and rolls out of the room.

"Oh Boo Boo! He might have had some other information!" I advise.

Good fortune smiles on Pedrock

After the wedding massacre I inherited the entire Grubweed fortune and estate as the remaining male relative.

Mr Cedric Evening-Star, the family lawyer who has been working on my behalf, sold the Grubweed family home and helped me arrange the funerals for Grandpa, Aunt Grubweed, Cornelius, Prunella and Estelle. Of course, Mr Wormhole the vicar was unable to perform the services on account of him fleeing the area in fear of his life, so a replacement, called Mr Fishwick, was brought in from a nearby village. He did a very nice job.

Mrs Charm decided to leave the village of Darkwound and is moving to Tintagel in Cornwall to continue the phenomenal success of her Medieval Horrors. She left me several of her chutney recipes and a plot outline for her next novel, *The Severed Leg*.

I left the ship building firm of Winkhood & Son and have bought myself an enormous boat which I have named *Dragonfly*. I intend to sail across the world in it. I have so much time before me and it is all my own. Indigo waters and cotton-wool-cloud skies of nothingness. Miss Penny Seashell and I are to be married at sea this very week. She is my "someone" to share all this freedom with, all this wonder.

While my sister slices up London in a butterfly dance of blades, I am sailing away into calmness, into an ocean of sleep.

Mr Angelcakes in London

I am having such fun here. Such fun! I am eating skin and it has made me so much stronger. My rotting skin is no longer rotting. No more brown teeth, green lips and heaps of squashed, mushy intestines.

I can move about London as a gentleman. Strawberry blond hair, ice-cream smile, bright eyes, top hat. I am tall and respectable looking. I am recovered, I am whole again.

But the only thing I can eat are skins. My dietary requirements have made me a serial killer. I catch them at night. Hook them under my arms in back-alleys. Entice them with gold coins. Watch them wriggle, squirm and squeal with horror in the ink-splat darkness.

"Don't eat that! It's alive!"

I eat and I wait. I am waiting for Boo Boo to retrieve the Angel-Eater. It will be returned to me. And also, I suppose, I miss her. My little butterfly.

My
little
butter
f
l
y

Detective Sergeant White and Constable Walnut in the Romney Marshes

The Romney Marshes are dotted with soft and silver moths that fly round our carriage. One lands on Constable Walnut's hand and sticks itself to him affectionately.

Detective Waxford and Boo Boo are to stay in London and investigate the Dancing Imp Theatre, whilst I and Walnut are here on the marshlands to view the Hummingbird family home and see if we can get any further information regarding the case. Mr Loveheart has taken it upon himself to locate Mr Angelcakes, a man neither Detective Waxford or myself have yet encountered, but who is leaving a trail of corpses throughout London – without their skins.

Hummingbird Manor House lies in the remotest part of the marshlands. A tiny church surrounded by plump sheep sits a half mile away from it. As our carriage pulls up to the main gates, a ewe raises her head from grazing and stares at us rather intently, eyeballs like soft boiled eggs.

"That sheep's looking at me!" Walnut says, rather worriedly.

"Don't encourage her," I sigh, and we step from the carriage.

Hummingbird Manor is a large sandy-coloured house, plain featured but with a large stone butterfly engraved over the main door. An elderly butler appears from the side entrance trundling a suitcase with what appears to be all his belongings.

"Hello there. I am Detective Sergeant White from Scotland Yard and this is Constable Walnut. I have a warrant to inspect the house."

The butler – whose face, on closer inspection, resembles a turnip – sneers. "There be no one to show ye about the house. The master is dead. Servants gone. I'm off too."

"That's fine. If you can just give me the key. It saves Walnut from kicking in the door."

The butler removes a large rusty-looking key from his coat pocket and hands it to me.

"If I may ask you some questions before you leave?"

"I don't know noffin," he replies.

"We'll see. What's your name?"

"Thangus Itch."

"Sorry?"

"Thangus Itch," he repeats.

"Unusual. How long have you worked for Ignatius Hummingbird?"

"I have been the butler in this house since the boys were born. Nearly sixty year."

"We are currently investigating a case which involves Ignatius Hummingbird and the kidnapping of women for a cult in London. It seems he kept a local woman in a cage in his basement. Do you know anything about this?"

"I don't know noffin about that."

"Never seen anything suspicious? Women being dragged into carriages, screaming, him hitting them over the head to knock them unconscious?"

"Nope."

"Anything you can tell me about Ignatius at all?"

"Master kept himself to himself."

"That's incredibly helpful," I say sourly. "Have you ever heard of the Butterfly Club?"

"Nope."

"One more thing Mr Itch. I would like to inspect your luggage before you leave the premises."

He looks startled. "Why?"

"You might have nicked something," Walnut interjects.

"I ain't letting you poke your nose into my stuff." Mr Itch spits on the ground.

"Walnut, hold him fast while I take a look." Walnut grabs the butler by the scruff of his neck while I open the case. A human foot rests neatly on top of a pile of laundry.

"Would you like to explain why there is a human foot in your bag?"

"Nope."

"Walnut, handcuff him to the carriage while we search the rest of the house."

"With pleasure, sir!"

I enter the key into the lock and turn it. The door swings gently open to reveal a sombre-looking interior. A huge portrait of Ignatius and Gabriel Hummingbird stands in the hallway glaring down upon me. Behind them is an Aztec temple, surrounded by butterflies. It is a bizarre painting.

Thangus Itch is laughing loudly from outside.

"Shut it!" Walnut shouts.

"Tick tock!" Mr Itch shouts manically back.

I pause. "What does he mean, tick tock?"

"Bomb," says Walnut.

We run outside. The house explodes, the front door flying off and bouncing against Thangus Itch, flattening him. I am thrown into the gates and Walnut flies past me into the field, landing next to the sheep. The house is an inferno, the air filled with dust spreading out into the marshlands.

When I regain consciousness I wake to see the sheep licking Walnut's face.

"Are you alright, Walnut?" I shout.

"Yes, sir," he replies.

I stand up. There is nothing left of the house. Thangus Itch is dead, squashed by the door. I walk over to Walnut who is sitting next to the insolent lump of a sheep. I extend a hand to him and help him up from the ground.

"So, what's the plan, sir?"

I look around us and out at the marshlands.

"We'll search that church over there," I say, pointing a finger, "and then we return to London."

The pair of us, half blown up, stroll the half mile over the marshlands through grazing sheep and brown and grey butterflies, which swoop delicately over our heads. The earth is soft under our feet, the squidge and squash of bogland. The church is tiny, painted white, with a huge keyhole in the door. The key to the Hummingbird Manor House is still in my pocket. It fits perfectly into the church lock.

"As I thought, this church belongs to the Hummingbird family. We may find a clue yet, Walnut."

The door swings open.

"Oh my God."

Walnut faints. A nearby sheep bleats rather sarcastically.

The church is stuffed to the brim with skeletons and decaying body parts. Green flesh hanging off, leaking eye sockets. The stench is unbearable. It nearly knocks me over. I gag and feel dizzy.

And round the walls of the church are painted butterflies of a thousand different colours, each one glittering with alien beauty. I shut the door and pass out in an undignified heap on the grass.

Detective Waxford and Boo Boo investigate the Dancing Imp Theatre

It's nearly midnight. Boo Boo and I are hiding behind the stage curtain of the Dancing Imp Theatre. I've got my gun and the little lady has her blades. The theatre is a ruin, the walls half collapsed. A tatty poster of *A Midsummer's Night Dream*, starring Lavender Charm as Titania, hangs off the wall.

I'm sure Detective White and Constable Walnut's investigations in the Romney Marsh have been uneventful. Nothing there but a load of sheep.

Suddenly there's a noise from the side of the theatre: the sound of a carriage. And in step two men carrying a body, and behind them the eye-patched Mr Cobweb ordering them about. The men dump the body on the stage and then go off to retrieve another.

The body is of a young woman. Her chest has

been cut open. An empty red space where her heart should be.

I signal to Boo Boo and we step out onto the stage. I aim my gun at Mr Cobweb's head. Boo Boo launches her blades, one each landing in the forehead off the hired thugs. They fall to the ground rather neatly. She steps lightly over to them and pulls the blades out, pressing her foot against their skulls as leverage; slightly disturbing considering she's only sixteen.

"Mr Cobweb," I say. "Nice to see you again. Fan of the theatre, are you?"

Mr Cobweb, a little surprised, says, "Shit."

"Would you care to explain to me the corpse on the stage?"

"Not especially."

I shoot him in the knee and he screams.

"Let's try that again, shall we?" Boo Boo stands next to him, her blade tapping gently on his shoulder.

"Boo Boo and I would very much like to visit the Butterfly Club and I believe you will be taking us there. Or she'll chop your arms off."

"This is really a pointless exercise, Detective Waxford. You have no idea what you're getting yourself into. Torture me all you wish…"

Boo Boo slices his arm off. It *plumps* to the floor.

"There was really no need for that!" he says through gritted teeth.

"Where is the Butterfly Club?" I ask again.

"This is ridiculous."

"It's not my arm lying on the floor."

Boo Boo places her blade on his other arm.

"Stop that!"' he cries.

"I am losing my patience. You know what I want, Mr Cobweb? I want to retire to a nice little cottage in the countryside. Relax. Write my memoirs. Maybe get a cat. Before I can do that, Mr Cobweb, I have to provide justice to this poor woman," (and I look towards the stage) "and the countless other women being kidnapped and murdered by your associates. If it takes cutting off every single part of your anatomy to retrieve the information I require then I will do it."

Boo Boo raises her blade.

"Houses of Parliament," he says softly.

"What?"

"The Butterfly Club is underneath the Houses of Parliament."

PART FOUR

It's a full moon tonight. Why am I not surprised? Lightning cracks across the sky, exploding and sizzling a church rooftop. The London nightscape boils above our heads.

Mr Cobweb, Boo Boo and I are dressed in black hooded robes and we are outside the entrance to the Butterfly Club, situated underneath the Houses of Parliament. I have my gun against Mr Cobweb's back in case he tries any funny business. I never thought I would see the day when I would be dressed up looking like this. It's frankly bloody embarrassing. Infiltrating a cult!

An enormous bare-chested man guards the entrance. He must be the size of a tree.

"Good evening, Mr Cobweb," he says, tipping his hat.

Mr Cobweb nods. "I have some guests with me this evening."

"Very good, sir," and he lets us through. I am hoping no one notices Mr Cobweb has only one arm. We left it in the Dancing Imp Theatre, lying on the floor.

We enter a long candlelit corridor and begin to descend a series of winding stairs which spirals far into the earth, under the Thames. On the walls, a series of tiny blue butterflies dance and shimmer in spirals. I can hear faint music and chanting deep beneath us.

"You do understand," says Mr Cobweb, "when they realise who you both are, they'll probably eat you alive."

I slap him round the back of his hooded head. "No one's eating me tonight. Especially while I'm wearing this stupid robe."

"I think you look rather fetching, Detective Waxford," says Boo Boo.

"I can't take myself seriously wearing this."

"If you want to blend in, you'll have to chant," Mr Cobweb interjects.

I slap him round the back of the head again.

"Suit yourself."

Further and further down we go. The walls are

cold stone, the butterflies are intermingled with bloody hand prints. The chanting becomes louder, the music some sort of hypnotic repetition. And finally we emerge into what I can only describe as an enormous Aztec temple, the size of St Paul's Cathedral. There must be five hundred hooded robed figures swaying and chanting; a sea of black. At the far end of this bizarre temple, a huge stone altar soaked in blood. And sitting behind, on a throne of human skulls, sits the prime minister, Zedock Heap. Above his head the Angel-Eater, with a pin through its heart. Its wings beat frantically.

"Well bugger me!" I say. "The leader of this demented cult is the *prime minister*."

"I thought you would have guessed by now," says Mr Cobweb, adjusting his hood.

"I have to arrest the British prime minister for running a death cult. I'm never going to get my pension."

"Probably not."

"Why the hell is he even involved?"

"He's a very powerful demon. He eats human hearts; they increase his power."

"Didn't Loveheart tell you?" says Boo Boo.

"NO, HE DID NOT TELL ME THE PRIME MINISTER WAS A DEMON. I bloody voted for him!"

"We all did."

"Why are all these people even here?"

"It's a bit like the Masons, really," Mr Cobweb continues happily.

I slap him round the back of the head again. "It's nothing like the fucking Masons. They don't kill people and eat body parts!"

"Detective Waxford," says Boo Boo. "Please can you free the butterfly for me?" and she points to the Angel-Eater.

"I'll try, sweetheart. I'm in shock at the moment."

We move to the very back of the temple, near an enormous pillar. Round the walls are huge, weird paintings of the Angel-Eater butterfly, liquorice black-winged, soaring over the ceiling.

And then we hear a scream and a young woman is dragged from the back of the temple and pulled onto the altar and tied down. Zedock Heap rises from his throne, moving towards her, a black dagger in his hands.

There is no time left.

I shoot my pistol at the ceiling. All five hundred hooded figures turn, gazing at me. Zedock Heap raises his head, curious.

"I am Detective Waxford of Scotland Yard and you're all nicked!"

Boo Boo uncovers her blades and positions herself in front of me. Mr Cobweb creeps aside. And then Zedock Heap, smiling to himself, shouts across the temple.

"COME TO ME," he says and the walls shake, ooze blood.

I shout back: "BOO BOO! WIPE THE FLOOR WITH THEM!"

Walnut and I have just returned to Scotland Yard where a note has been pinned to my desk.

Percival,

Butterfly Club under Houses of Parliament. Boo Boo and I already there. QUITE POSSIBLY DEAD. Hurry Up!

Waxford

"Let's get to it, Walnut!"

"Yes, sir!"

We race outside and hail the nearest cabbie. "Quick as you can. Houses of Parliament."

"Yes, guv'ner."

Our carriage races along the streets of London. The moon is full tonight and wicked.

"Eventful day so far," says Walnut.

I load my pistol. Walnut holds up the hand grenade Mr Loveheart gave him for Christmas, shaped like a potato, a little red heart painted on it.

"Could prove useful," he says.

The cabbie drops us off and we circle round the back of the Houses of Parliament to where an enormous man stands guarding a small door, obscured from view by the shadows. We approach him.

"Can I help you gentlemen?" he says, carefully.

"Open the door. I am Detective Sergeant White and I am investigating a series of murders."

"No," he replies coolly.

I take my pistol out. "Earlier today my constable and I were blown up. I'm not in the mood for the word 'no' tonight."

"You'll have to shoot me."

"Fair enough." And so I do, albeit in the leg.

We enter the building and follow the staircase downwards, following the noises of screaming and gunfire. Finally we enter the enormous temple. A body part (I can't distinguish exactly what part) flies past my head. Walnut and I stand there for a moment, dumbfounded.

Waxford runs towards the altar, shooting hooded

figures left right and centre. We hear him swearing loudly and as he proceeds to push his way towards what appears to be–

"That's the prime minister," says Walnut, interrupting my thoughts. "And it looks like Detective Waxford is attempting to shoot him."

Boo Boo is slicing her way through a mass of black hooded bodies. The floor is soaked with blood and body parts. It's like watching a demented butterfly soar about.

"She's very graceful," says Walnut, as Boo Boo slices an acolyte in half. We both duck as the upper half of the body is thrown screaming towards us, hitting the wall with an undignified thud.

Detective Waxford and Boo Boo are now at the far end of the temple, either side of Zedock Heap. The remaining mass of crazed black hooded figures starts running towards Walnut and me.

I raise my pistol and aim.

Walnut takes out the pin, throws the hand grenade.

BOOM!

Mr Loveheart versus Mr Angelcakes

Well it's a lovely evening for hunting down Mr Angelcakes. Milk and butter stars, a cheesecake moon. And I'm dressed in a rather fetching shade of peach. I can smell Mr Angelcakes: black slime and glitter dust. The smell of a magic dead thing.

Follow the trail of eaten skins.

I seem to have ended up down a fish-stink alley round the back of a pub. A group of vegetable-faced men – flat caps and big pork hands – eyeballing me.

"Queer!" one of them shouts.

"Excuse me?" I reply.

"You heard me, you weirdo," the thing with a potato head replies.

I walk up to them, a group of four huddled together, tobacco-brown teeth, yellow eyes, as many teeth as brain cells.

"Were you attempting to insult me?"

"Sling your hook or you'll get a slap."

I pull my silver pistol out and rest it on his forehead. "And you will feel your brain all over the wall."

One of them picks up a rock and tries to sneak up behind me.

I leave them all dead in the alleyway.

Whoops.

Higgledy-piggledy, zig-zagging side alleys. I move towards the treacle ooze river and then I see him. He's standing over the body of a man, devouring a skin. Blood splattered all down his lovely waistcoat.

"Hello, Mr Angelcakes."

He looks at me rather strangely.

"Hello, Mr Loveheart."

"I see you are enjoying your time in London. The capital does have a lot to offer. Excellent theatre, fashion and sightseeing, and of course occasional cannibalism."

"I like your skin."

"I'm afraid I'm rather attached to it."

"I like your skin," and he steps closer to me

I have a little homemade bomb in my pocket. It

has a red loveheart on it. A bomb of love.

I grab hold of him. Shove it into his mouth.

Tickety tock!

He explodes. All over me! Completely ruined my peach waistcoat. What a mess! I peel off a large piece of greenish skin which is lying over my face and plop it onto the floor. I make my way out of the little dark alley.

And then Death appears.

"Mr Loveheart. If you could just run a little errand for me?"

"Do I have time to change first? I need a little freshening up," I say, brushing what appears to be an eyeball hanging from my sleeve.

"No."

"Fine," I say sulkily.

"Get to the House of Parliament. Zedock Heap's running a cult."

"Do you know how difficult it is to find a cab this time of night!"

A lightning bolt hits the street and *puff!* A magnificent white horse, as white as ice-cream dreams, suddenly appears next to Death.

"Get on the horse, Mr Loveheart. Be the hero."

I pat the horse's nose and he whinnies. "And how

did you acquire this supernatural horse exactly?"

"I borrowed him," sighs Death.

"From whom?"

"The old gods."

"You mean you've stolen him."

"Borrowed!" repeats Death, exasperated.

"Very well. I accept your proposal."

"Get on the horse, Mr Loveheart."

And so I do. "Do you want to come with me? Have some fun?"

"No. I am already stretching the rules for you, Loveheart. And, frankly, I'm knackered."

Riding across London on a white horse. This horse is simply marvellous. I gallop into the night of London, down the streets. People stop and stare. Goggle with disbelief. I must fizzle like weird magic. I look like a prince galloping into the rat tail, ink splodge London, faster and faster. Eyes on stalks: they watch us whizz past.

I am lost deep within the book of a fairytale.

Fizzy whizzzzzzzzzzzzzzzzzzzzzz.

Boo Boo slices and dices

Chop chop choppity chop chop
chop chop
chop chop
CHOP
CHOP
CHOP
CHOP
CHOP
CHOP
CHOP
CHOP

Zedock Heap and the butterfly

She really is impressive. Little killing machine. BUTTERFLY GIRL. She's killed most of my followers, hacked them up neatly like chopping carrots. A pile of feet, arms and heads. She moves lightning fast, *ZOOM CHOP CHOP* as though suspended on a wire. I've never seen anything like her before. Maybe I should set her on fire. Or whip her up like egg whites. Make a meringue of her.

A bomb has just exploded, my remaining followers blown up, limbs scattered over the walls of my temple. Well, that's a little embarrassing.

And here she comes, the little butterfly landing in front of me, and alongside her a rather manic looking Detective Waxford aiming a gun above my head. He shoots at the Angel-Eater; the glass shatters and it emerges. Liquorice wings soar across the ceiling and dive towards Boo Boo.

Zoom into her, like a ghost. They merge.

LIGHTNING BOLT.

She's hit.

She's opening her blades to me. Offering me an ending.

"Now this really has been fun but the game is over," I look down upon them both.

Detective Waxford moves closer to me. "Zedock Heap. I am arresting you for mass murder, cannibalism and for running an unlicensed cult."

"You know, I'm very good friends with Queen Victoria."

"That's her problem," and he aims the gun at my head.

"You're all so entertaining." And I lift Detective Waxford into the air and fling him across my temple.

"SHHHHHIIIIIIIIITTTTTTTTTTTTTTTTTTTTTTT TTTTTTTTTTTT!!!!!!"

He bounces against a pillar and slithers into a crumpled heap on the floor.

The butterfly girl runs her blade through me. It feels like a tiny spider kiss. I grab her by the hair and pull her to me. Pull the blade out. Hold it to her throat.

Detective Waxford, still alive, fires a bullet into my head.

I squeeze the walls of the temple. They're closing in with my magic. The temple wobbling, the ceiling breaking apart. I fling the butterfly girl across the temple, SMASH HER INTO THE WALL.

And I am laughing. I AM LAUGHING amidst the mountain of body parts and corpses.

"I AM THE MASTER OF YOU ALL."

A horse whinnies. In rides Mr Loveheart on a gigantic white stallion. Well, there's an entrance!

"COME TO ME, LITTLE PRINCE!"

Loveheart and Zedock

My horse has leapt into the temple. Marvellous entrance, I waggle my sword about. Ooooooh look at the heaps of dead bodies! LOOK AT THE MESS. MARVEL AT THE GOO!

I slice up and few more nutty acolytes. I ride past Detective White and Walnut who are hiding behind a pillar and they wave at me as I gallop past. A foot flies past my head!

Tally-ho!

Boo Boo is picking herself up off the floor, Waxford lying on the ground surrounded and shooting every which way.

Zedock Heap is sitting upon his throne of skulls waiting for me. I ride up to his bloodied altar and point my sword at him.

"And here we are again, Mr Loveheart." He opens

his hands like a book. Are there magic words written on his hands?

My horse rears and whinnies appropriately. DAZZLE *ZAP* SEE THE SPARK!

I dismount. I flash a brilliant smile. "You're about to retire, Zedock. Permanently," I say, and I slice my sword through air, dismantle molecules.

"COME TO ME," he grins. "I EAT LITTLE PRINCES."

And then I see him for what he really is, I see what is underneath his skin. Under the bones of him. I've seen it so many times. In so many things. In a world gone quite mad.

And I tell him, "We are the same, Zedock. You and I. We are the underneath. We are the same." And I am sad because I know I am mad and dangerous. I know how close to him I really am. What would it take to push me over the edge, into him, into his space?

"Come to me, little prince, let me feel your madness," and he puts his hand over my head and I let him in, I let him understand me.

HE HOLDS ME LIKE A DADDY.

He reads my thoughts, sees my dreams. Sees what I am made of, and it is electricity. It makes him shudder, unexpected. It makes him quiver.

ELECTRICAL VOLTAGE. He staggers a little under the blast of it, and stares at me dumfounded.

"Now you understand," I say. I chop his head off. Watch it bounce down the steps. *Boing! Bong! Splat!*

I can feel history replay itself; clocks move backwards and then jolt forward. Timelines shifts. Butterflies break out of glass frames and whizz into space. The world liquidizes. Evaporates. Becomes air.

There is so much screaming. Blood and body parts. And yet I am elsewhere. I am far away. In the melt of space, on the edges of timelines waiting for the world to re-form, spin again and dissolve in a fraction of a second. Over and over. Round and round. There is no end.

I am the Lord of the Underworld and I will always be on the edge of the world. I will always be on the edges.

I peer through a telescope and laugh at the dead. I laugh because I see human souls; see them fly into space. See them burst. Turn into stars.

I lift beautiful Boo Boo onto my horse, kiss her. MAKE HER MINE.

I hold the head of Zedock Heap aloft.

Zedock Heap is a splatty mess. The temple is a heap of body parts.

Waxford is kicking the corpse.

"Detective Waxford. Are you alright?"

"I'm fucking marvellous," and he kicks him again, staring mad-eyed down at the corpse, "Zedock Heap – I'm fucking arresting you."

Detective White thankfully intervenes and puts his arm round Waxford's shoulder. "He's dead, Waxford. It's over."

Oh dear, poor Waxford. I think he's in shock.

I put my arms round Boo Boo. "My lady, I believe it's time for us to ride off into the moonlight."

"Have we got a happy ending, Mr Loveheart?" she says.

"Of course, my lady. I happen to be on very good terms with the authoress."

August 1889
THE BAG OF TRIPE PUB, WHITECHAPEL

Detective Sergeant White has organised a retirement party for Waxford. Isn't that charming?

This pub is a curious hole. Smells of meat pie and something dead. A gloomy cavern of ragtag pickpockets, putrid corpse smugglers and Scotland Yard detectives.

I have, of course, got a card and a present for Waxford. I inspect my thoughtful, well-chosen card, which has an illustration of a decapitated head on a stick. Inside it reads in beautiful red ink:

> *Dear Waxford,*
>
> *Congratulations! You are not dead.*
>
> *Love from Me ☙ & Boo Boo*
> *xxxxxxxxxxxxxxxxxxxxxxxxxxxxxx*

The present is a preserved stuffed foot I obtained from a student medical doctor. I've wrapped a pink ribbon round it with a heart-shaped gift tag. He will *love* it!

It's 8 o'clock in the evening when Boo Boo and I arrive in this quaint little part of Whitechapel. A corpse decomposes quietly in a back alley. The moon is a sky lantern; the stars a-fizzle.

A few turnip-faced locals lurk in the corners of this establishment. A bow-legged folk singer has been hired for the occasion, singing a song about fish and bearded men. He taps his spindly foot against the floor, beating out a rhythm. I throw a chair at him, knocking him out cold with a squeal.

Rufus Hazard, who's leaning over the bar chatting up the barmaid, responds, rather inebriated: "Good shot, Loveheart! I was about to punch him in the face."

"What do you think you're playing at, Loveheart?" shouts White, who's standing with Waxford and Walnut. Walnut's holding a scotch egg the size of a head on a cocktail stick.

"What deviltry is that?" I point my sword at the scotch egg.

"Homemade," smiles Walnut.

"By whom?"

Walnut points at the pub landlord who's wiping a pint glass with a dirty rag. He smiles nervously at me. "Speciality of the pub. It's perfectly normal, I swear!"

Boo Boo draws her blades.

Waxford shouts, happy on whisky, "You two stop mucking about. Come over here."

A selection of finger foods lies across the bar. Is that another scotch egg I spy? Mmm, some curious potted-meat sandwiches and mini-quiches. I inspect them for bombs.

Boo Boo runs over to Pedrock and his fiancée, Miss Seashell, who have appeared. Gives her brother a big cuddle. He has a marvellous boat I hear, an insecty delight.

I sneak up on Waxford, who's helping the concussed folk singer rise from the floor.

"Happy Retirement." I hand him the gift.

He looks at it with suspicion. "Hmm-mmm, what is THIS I wonder?" and unwraps it. "A preserved foot! How considerate of you."

Walnut peers over his shoulder. "Symbol of good luck, that is."

"What the hell are you talking about?" Waxford shouts.

"It's well known," Walnut continues with a

remarkably serious expression, "that in some primitive cultures a foot would be hung outside the front door to encourage prosperity, a ripe old age and virility."

Waxford slaps Walnut in the face. "STOP IT! I'm surrounded by insane people!"

"Come now, Waxford," I smile my best smile, "You've had fun."

Waxford puts the foot on the bar. The barman examines it with a concerned interested. "What are you bloody looking at?" he screams.

Detective White puts his arm on Waxford's shoulder. "We shall miss you, Henry."

The folk singer, whom I've kept my eye upon, has removed himself to the corner of the room and sheepishly sips his lime cordial. If he so much as hums, I will beat him to death with the giant scotch egg.

Rufus staggers over towards me and shouts "I'M WATCHING YOU!" to the folk singer, who squeaks in fear.

"You and I," continues Rufus, pissed as a newt, "understand one another, dear boy. We both have a sensitive appreciation of the arts. I once saw a mime act in Paris. I strangled the fellow half to death with my bare hands. Slippery bugger got away through an invisible window, but he learnt a valuable lesson that day."

"Which was?" Detective White interjects.

"Not to PRAT about on the streets in a leotard. As a proud Englishman, I won't tolerate that nonsense. I should have taken my belt to his backside."

Detective White coughs and raises his pint glass. "A TOAST. To HENRY WAXFORD, the finest man I have ever worked with. The bravest. Scotland Yard's best and brightest. To Waxford!"

"Waxford!" we all say and sink back our drinks.

The folk singer opens his mouth.

"DON'T YOU DARE!" Rufus cries, and takes off his belt. His trousers fall down around his ankles.

And they all live happily ever after…

MRS CHARM

I have just returned from a book signing in Edinburgh. Lovely people, wonderful shortbread. *The Severed Leg*, my most recent novel, has been a marvellous success. I have sent Mr Loveheart several signed copies of my books and he always sends me the most charming letters back.

My Dear Mrs Charm,

As always, you woo me with your wicked tales.
'The Severed Leg' is a particular favourite of mine.
I was especially fond of the chapter with the jars of
Saints' toes in formaldehyde – what a beautiful
touch!
    Today I have decided to play a little prank on

Detective Waxford. I am writing this letter whilst hiding in a bush outside his cottage. He's retired, you know – recovering from a nervous breakdown in the sleepy village of Wugglethump, in Kent. He has a cat too, called Mr Lumpy – it is very fat and it is staring at me with its beady eyes!!!!

I miss Detective Waxford.

So I am going to throw a corpse through his window. I dug one up from the graveyard.

I will let you know how it goes!

Love, your dear friend,

Mr JohnLoveheart 🦌

Oh, isn't he a sweetie? So thoughtful.

I've got a new batch of chutney on the stove: fig and cherry with a dash of sage. Excellent cure for flatulence. I do love it here in Tintagel and I have even acquired a handsome admirer, Mr Horace Sunbeam, a red-haired retired Professor of medieval literature. He is taking me out for tea and cake tomorrow. The Victoria sponge cake is very good at Mrs Gobble's Tearooms. And he writes me the most beautiful poetry, wrapped up in bunches of forget-me-nots, and puts them outside my door.

I'm loved and I love, and that is all any one of us can hope for.

PEDROCK

My ship, the *Dragonfly,* has brought me so much happiness. Penny and I are married now, under wobbly stars and a sea full of fish. Together we will sail across the oceans, the great flat mirrors of the world.

My love and I.

My love and I and *Dragonfly.*

RUFUS HAZARD

Loveheart gave me Zedock's throne of skulls. It's in my library and I'm sitting in it drinking a brandy and reading my daily horoscope in the *Times Psychic Supplement,*

> *LEO*
> *Today is excellent for gardening and spending quality time with root vegetables, especially those of the parsnip family.*

I put the paper down, write my own prediction. Pluck up my quill.

> *Today you will sit on a giant throne of skulls and pretend that you are Ruler of the Universe!*

MR OTTO INK-SQUID

My bloody shop burnt down. I'm going to complain to the authoress. Where's *my* happy ending? Fifty Ouija boards and a box full of tarot cards went up in flames. What have I learnt from this story? Don't try to predict the future.

I make lodgings at the Pear Tree tavern for the evening and a small, very sinister looking child arrives with a package.

"Mr Ink-Squid?"

"Yes," I reply.

"Compensation," and he hands me a parcel.

His eyes, I note, are black stars. I untie the package. Inside is a large silver key.

"Congratulations. You are now the owner of a large, moated castle."

"Who was the previous owner?"

"Professor Hummingbird. I believe you have heard of him. He was a deranged mass-murdering occultist. Impaled on his wedding day."

"Oh. Thank you very much."

"The pleasure is all mine."

PANDORA

A man called Mr Loveheart came and took me away from the asylum. Took me away in his magic coach to the fairyland of Cornwall.

I am staying with Titania, Queen of the Fairies, who makes very nice chutney. I am knitting scarves, rainbow colours, miles long. I am inside out with happiness.

Detective Sergeant White and Constable Walnut down the pub

Constable Walnut and I are in the Nag's Head, having a few pints.

"I think I've gone a bit peculiar," says Walnut.

"You've only just realised that?"

"It's the beer. Bit frothy. I have quite a delicate stomach."

"Really."

"Yes. It's because I have psychic ability. I'm sensitive to dark auras."

"Speaking of dark auras, it's your round, Walnut."

"The barmaid frightens me. She keeps giving me the eye."

"Off you go, Walnut, no excuses."

Walnut slopes off. The barmaid leans her enormous bosom on the bar and winks at him suggestively. He returns rather quickly with two pints of brown froth.

"She's predatory," and he nervously sits back down.

"I have some interesting news. I received a letter from Detective Waxford this morning. He thanked us for the retirement gift," I say sarcastically.

"Oh shit, I forgot about that."

"Yes. I thought you might, considering I sent you out specifically to get him a book of William Blake's poetry and you decided to choose something yourself."

"In my defence…"

"Yes, I'm waiting."

"I was really hungover."

"Walnut, you sent him a book instructing how to perform lobotomies. And even worse than that, you inscribed it with the lines 'I hope this helps you recover'."

"I thought it might provide him with some insight into how to deal with criminals, sir."

"By removing their brains?"

"It's a valid theory, sir."

"So, you sent Detective Waxford – a man who has served Scotland Yard for over twenty five years, won countless medals for bravery – a book about how to remove a brain from a skull."

"You think it's not quite appropriate?"

"No, it's not appropriate."

"Um… so what did his letter say, exactly?"

"You really want to know?"

"Not really."

I take the letter out of my coat pocket and give Walnut a deeply penetrating stare.

Dear Percival and Walnut,

What can I say? A book about lobotomy… I presume you chose this, Walnut. What a thoughtful gift. I was deeply moved. My brain, however, will remain in my skull. But I can't guarantee Walnut's will when I see him next.

Waxford (and Mr Lumpy the cat)

The Angel-Eater

I'm only a symbol.

Hang me on a wall. Pin me through my heart.
Paint me on a temple.

The only power I have

        is

            what

                  you

                        give

                              me.

Detective Waxford and Mr Lumpy the cat

Next time I see Walnut, I am going to hit him over the head with a welding mallet.

It's very peaceful here in Wugglethump. Nice spot of Kent. Apple trees in my garden, wild plums and floppy headed daises. How happy I am. I love you, daisies!

I've just finished reading one of Mrs Charm's medieval horrors, *The Curse of Black-Stump Priory*. Mr Lumpy quite enjoyed it. Involved some sort of black magic rituals going on in the cellars: incantations, whippings, human sacrifice. That's the lovely part of being retired. I can read about the horror but I don't have to be involved any more. Beautiful detachment. Finally!

A decomposing corpse flies through my window and lands with a squelchy thud onto the carpet. I can hear laughing outside. I pick up my gun and run to the window.

"MR LOVEHEART! I AM GOING TO BLOODY SHOOT YOU!"

And he appears smiling at the window, dressed in lemon meringue yellow. "Waxford! Happy Retirement. Aren't you going to invite me in for tea and cake?"

"I AM SUPPOSED TO BE RECOVERING FROM A NERVOUS BREAKDOWN. WHAT THE HELL DO YOU THINK YOU ARE PLAYING AT?"

"I missed you."

"SEND ME A FUCKING POSTCARD THEN. DON'T THROW A CORPSE THROUGH MY WINDOW."

"Oh come on now, Waxford. I know you're pleased to see me."

"WHAT THE FUCK AM I SUPPOSED TO DO WITH THIS?" I scream, waving the gun at the corpse.

"You could examine it for any criminal interference?"

"IT'S ALREADY BEEN CRIMINALLY INTERFERED WITH. YOU DUG HIM UP! GET RID OF IT NOW OR I WILL KILL YOU." And I aim the gun at his head.

"Oooh, you spoilsport." Mr Loveheart climbs through the window, picks the dead body up by its decomposing foot and begins to drag it out of the front door.

I slam the door shut and peer out of the window. "I'm watching you, Loveheart," and I waggle the gun at him. He drags the body down the path and rolls it into a ditch, comes back into my house and slumps himself down in the armchair. He sighs. "I'm so bored."

Mr Lumpy jumps onto his lap and purrs. The traitor!

"I am not providing you with entertainment, Loveheart. Go and play with Detective White and Constable Walnut."

"But you're funnier. If I prod you, you squeak!"

"You're not going to leave, are you?"

"No," he smiles, and he strokes Mr Lumpy affectionately.

Boo Boo

I live with Mr Loveheart in his mansion of hearts.
They are all over the place. There's even one on the
privy.

We dance round his house like mad bugs.

He dances round my heart.

Me and the mad prince.

Hand in heart, heart in hand. ❦

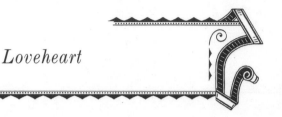

Loveheart

I walk my gardens. Make Underworld trees appear, red fruit bulge. Wobble and drop off. I lie on wet grass and gaze at the stars, try and count them. Lose track, start again and then fall asleep.

Snore.

Dream of the underneath.

I AM LORD OF THE UNDERWORLD,.

There are sharks swimming in my head. There are worlds spinning and breaking in my heart.

If you kiss me

        you

            will

                live

                    forever.

Death

What colour is the devil? You're about to find out.

Epilogue
QUEEN VICTORIA

The answer to Death's question is *royal blue*.

It's a glorious morning; leaves the colour of blood spin outside the window and fall like splatters of a dissection on the grounds of the palace – as though the sky has been sliced with a razor. Is God perhaps a wicked doctor?

There's a delicate tapping on the door and in slips Mr Hours with his lopsided smile and broken teeth.

"Your Majesty," and he bows very low. Not low enough, in my opinion.

"What news, Mr Hours?"

"Some rather shocking information, I am afraid," he replies nervously.

I stare out of the window. "Continue."

"The Butterfly Club has been uncovered by Scotland Yard. All its members slaughtered. Zedock

Heap, the prime minister, decapitated."

"I see." But I want to crush the world in my fist. My beautiful Zedock. My beautiful Zedock. I stare out into my gardens; into blood roses. They melt, ooze across the lawn with my rage.

"We are aware who is responsible," he stutters.

"And WHO is responsible, Mr Hours?" My voice exerts a pressure that makes the glass crack in the windows.

Very quickly he takes out a little piece of paper from his jacket pocket: "Lord Loveheart chopped his head off."

I AM THE RAGE. I AM THE RAGE. I AM BOILING. The windows shatter. The gardener explodes. The blood fills the garden, seeps into the room, under my slippers. LOVEHEART, LOVEHEART, LOVEHEART, LOVEHEART, MY REVENGE will be a horror story. I will stop the earth moving. I will pull the planets down from the sky.

I WILL EAT YOU ALIVE!

"But," Mr Hours continues trembling, "he was helped by… let me see: a *Detective Henry Waxford, Detective Sergeant Percival White, Constable Walnut and Miss Boo Boo Frogwish.*"

The blood continues to fill the palace.

"I want them squashed. I want to place my foot on them and squash them into the ground."

"An excellent suggestion, ma'am," he stutters.

"Oh, and Mr Hours."

"Yes?"

"I am very displeased."

He gives me a crumbling look, as though evaporating from existence. "I really am most terribly sorry, Your Majesty."

It shouldn't come as a surprise really. Men always disappoint me. And he withers away out of the room, leaving me in standing in blood. Leaving me with my rage.

I stare into space. Into your little world. Into the hole of you. The blood rises, wets my skirts, ruins the hem line. My anger is cosmic, if you felt it you would go mad, your brains would melt under its energy.

I am your Queen, I am your Queen. Your Mother, England.

Come and give me a cuddle. Let me squeeze the air from you.

LET ME BREAK EVERY BONE IN YOU.

I scream and the Palace shakes. The chandelier explodes. Big Ben falls over.

Timelines fragment. The planets wobble in the cosmos.

LOVEHEART, Loveheart, Loveheart.

Little Loveheart, you think you can send me back to Hell?

**I AM
BEYOND
ALL
STARS.**

Acknowledgments

BIG thank yous to Bryony my agent, John Coulthart for the covers, Phil my editor, Marc for book design, and the other Angry Robots. Also, a cheeky mention to Matt Berry & chocolate for making the world more joyful.

About the author

Ishbelle Bee writes horror and loves fairy tales, the Victorian period (especially top hats!), and cake tents at village fêtes (she believes serial killers usually opt for the Victoria Sponge). She currently lives in Edinburgh. She doesn't own a rescue cat, but if she did his name would be Mr Pickles.

twitter.com/IshbelleBee